PISTOL DAISY

PISTOL DAISY BOOK 1

NATALIA LEIGH

Pistol Daisy

Natalia Leigh

This book is a work of fiction. All names, places, characters, and events are products of the author's imagination and are fictitious. Any similarities to actual events, places, or people, living or dead, is coincidental.

Enchanted Ink Publishing
PO Box 620652
Littleton CO, 80162

First Edition: June 2020

Paperback ISBN: 978-1-7326782-3-1
eBook ISBN: 978-1-7326782-4-8
Library of Congress Control Number: 2019939350

Printed in the United States of America

Enchanted Ink Publishing
www.enchantedinkpublishing.com

PISTOL DAISY SERIES

Pistol Daisy

Whiskey City

It's my birthday today. But I don't feel any older. None wiser, neither.

D. Allen

CHAPTER 1
August 1880

I CAN SMELL the rain coming in, that delicate concoction of summer and earth and stone. The clouds are thick and gray, threatening an afternoon storm. I've been sitting here a while now, sketching the fawns that follow their mamas through the sparse yellow grass swaying in the breeze, and it's nearly time I headed home.

Billy lies beside me, his shirt open so the sun can kiss his summer-gold skin. I feel his eyes tracing the planes of my face as I sit hunched over my sketchbook. He reaches over to push his fingers through my tangled blond hair.

"Stop," I say, but I don't mean it, and he can tell. His fingertips trail down my neck, across my shoulder, down my back. I sigh softly at his touch, my pencil hesitating on the journal page. "I gotta finish this before that storm hits."

"Come here." He pushes up onto his forearms as I lean

down, and our lips meet hungrily, as if they weren't pressed together just an hour ago. On any other day I'd let him slip the shirt from my shoulders and place kisses down my chest, but not today. Today I've gotta get home to help Mama with my birthday supper, and I've gotta finish this sketch before the rain starts.

I push Billy away and he slumps into the grass with a displeased grunt. "Damn you, Daisy Allen."

Smiling, I finish my sketch as Billy buttons up his shirt and wipes the light sheen of sweat from his brow.

Our horses graze beside us. Lucky, my paint gelding, glistens under the afternoon sun, his coat gleaming from the bath I gave him this morning. It won't be long before he's coated in dirt again. Without fail, he'll go and get himself muddy almost as soon as I've cleaned him up. Billy's mare ain't no better. She has a few braids twisted into her mane— his little sister's doing, no doubt.

Billy lets out a sigh and runs a hand through his dark hair. I wonder, not for the first time, if I could see myself as his wife. I'm nineteen today, and plenty old enough to be married. Mama wants me to start looking for a husband— she don't know nothing about Billy—but I ain't sure I'm ready yet. Papa tells me to take my time, but I can see in Mama's eyes that she's worried about me. Every time I come in from helping Papa in the fields, with dirt under my nails and my brother Jacob's old shirt hanging off my shoulders, I see the concern in her eyes. She wants me settled down, with my own land and husband and home full of kids. But I still feel like a kid myself, and ain't no way I can see myself raising one.

A gust of wind blows dirt into my eyes, causing me to shield my face. Thunder rumbles overhead and the fawn I've been watching dashes to its mama's side, tucking itself under her front legs.

"Storm's 'bout to hit," Billy says. He pushes to his feet and reaches down to help me up. His hands are rough, calloused, and I know it's from helping Jacob fix all them fences earlier this week. I watched the two of them from a distance, wondering if my brother would pummel his friend if he found out what we do together in Billy's barn.

I close my sketchbook and drop it into the satchel slung across my shoulders. Billy's hair is windswept and his eyes are hungry as I pull him in for one last, long kiss.

As we part, his fingers play along the waistband of my jeans. "I've been thinkin'," he says, his forehead pressed to mine.

"That ain't good," I mumble.

He ignores my comment. "Maybe we should tell folks . . . about us."

When I pull away, his eyes are narrowed and serious.

"And you wanna do what? Court me proper?"

"I would, if that's what you want."

I glance away. He brought this up once before, and I laughed him into his clothes and right out of the barn. But this time feels different. We've been sneaking around like this for six months now, since the winter had us clinging to each other for warmth, and I know it can't go on forever, yet I ain't sure I want anything to change.

"Think about it," Billy says. He steps away, his lips quirking up into a smile. "But I ain't gonna wait around forever."

"You got suitors I don't know about?"

He doesn't answer, and the silence makes me bite my lip. There are plenty of young ladies in town in need of a husband. It wouldn't surprise me none if some of them had their eyes on him.

Billy swings up onto his mare and turns her away. "Happy birthday," he says, and then puts his heels to her flanks and they leave me standing there in the summer wind.

Lucky lifts his head when I pick up his reins, a mouthful of grass still dangling out the side of his lips. With practiced grace, I swing up onto his bare back and situate myself behind his withers. The herd of deer is watching me now, interested and wary. I turn Lucky toward home and give his sides a squeeze. He snorts, steps into a lazy trot, and then we're headed home for my birthday supper.

We've grown up on these plains, Lucky and I. When Papa brought him home years ago, I didn't want a thing to do with him. He'd gallop around the corral, causing a ruckus, kicking and biting if anyone got too close. But something in him saw something in me, and we bonded over apples stolen from Mama's kitchen and spring afternoons running through rainstorms. Papa taught me how to work with him, how to earn his respect, and how to give it in return. We've galloped all across this land, avoiding rattlers during the day and listening to the coyotes howling to the moon at night. The sounds of the plains are home to me, as is the feel of Lucky beneath me, his sturdy hooves carrying us for miles beneath an endless blue sky.

Thunder rumbles again, and sheets of rain are already falling over the hills in the distance. I wouldn't mind getting caught in the rain—I've always loved a good storm—but Mama will bake me into her next batch of corn bread if I'm late again.

Lucky lopes all the way home, his mane blowing in the wind. Our little farmhouse sits on a stretch of dry, flat land, and outbuildings surround it: a shed, the barn, an old doghouse that's been empty for years now. I still miss that hound. Papa does too, but he don't admit it. I know that's why he won't get another one. Losing them hurts too damn much.

Papa and Jacob are standing on the porch smoking cigarettes when I ride up. Jacob flicks ash into the dirt and gives me a smile as I slide down from Lucky's back. That smile has been known to break the hearts of young girls all over Rock Creek.

"Just in time," he says. "Mama's been watchin' out the window for ya."

"Supper's 'bout ready," Papa says. "I'll put him away." He reaches out and takes Lucky's reins from me. Before I head inside, Papa pulls me in for a brief hug and kisses me on the cheek. His beard is rough against my face, but I don't mind a bit. "Happy birthday," he says.

"Thanks, Papa." I smile at him, then steal a drag from Jacob's cigarette before knocking the dirt off my boots and heading into the house.

"Daisy?" Mama calls out. "That you?"

"Yes, Mama!"

She steps out of the kitchen, apron around her waist and her blond hair tied back in a low bun. From the top of my head to the ends of my toes, I'm my mother's child. I got her looks, her laugh, and her slim fingers, which are smeared with graphite from that sketch I finished earlier.

"Go and get yourself cleaned up," Mama says. "Then you can help me finish supper."

Mama pours me warm water from the kettle, and I dip a rag into the wash bowl and use it to clean my face, hands, and body. I wash Billy's kisses from my neck as I stare out the window across the rolling plains. His words echo in my head. What to do about them, I ain't quite sure.

When I'm clean and dressed in a fresh blouse and skirt, I join Mama in the kitchen. She tosses me an apron, accepts a kiss on the cheek, and puts me to work.

Moving around one another in the kitchen is like our own kind of dance—one we've done hundreds of times. Ain't no place in this house feel more like home than right here, standing beside Mama as we chop and stir and laugh.

We're near done when Mama props a hand on her hip and levels her blue eyes on me. I wipe flour from my hands as she continues to stare.

"What?" I ask, pushing a strand of hair away from my face with the back of a hand.

"I'm just gettin' a good look at you." She smiles, and I turn away shyly.

"Well stop it."

"I birthed you—I can look at you all I want."

Laughing, I roll my eyes and make to walk away, but Mama grabs my hand and turns me around.

"Nineteen," she says softly, as if to herself. "Can't believe my girl has grown up so fast." Her eyes grow glassy and I start to pull away.

"Don't you even think about cryin'," I say, struggling against her. "Ain't nobody like when you get all soft on 'em."

"Your birthday is the one day a year I'm allowed to get soft. Now you listen to me, Daisy Margaret Allen." She gives me a firm squeeze. "I want you to know that I love you, and I'm proud of you."

I stop struggling when she says that. Mama's always been hard on me, wanting me to be more this or less that. I've never felt that she's ashamed of me, necessarily, but I wouldn't say she's proud of me, neither. She especially weren't proud last Sunday when I ripped my best skirts racing some of the boys after church. But at least Lucky and I won—we ain't never been beat.

She trails a thumb across my cheek and gives me a tearful smile. "I just wanted you to know," she says.

"I know, Mama." I pull her in for a hug just as Papa and Jacob come in through the front door.

"You'd best not be trackin' mud through my house," Mama snaps, turning away from me to make sure the men aren't making a mess. And not a moment too soon—I'm able to wipe away the moisture that's come to my eyes before she can see how much her words mean to me.

We sit around the fire after supper, talking and laughing as the flames crackle. Papa's leaning back in a creaky wooden chair with a burning cigarette in one hand. The window beside him is open and fills the house with the smell of smoke, earth, and rain. The storm hit us during supper and ain't let up yet. Every so often lightning flashes across the sky, chasing away the shadows for a brief moment before darkness falls again.

"Wanna watch the rain?" I ask Jacob, and he's quick to agree. We push through the screen door and the air that greets us is cool and fresh. The top step is still dry, shielded from the rain by the tin roof overhead. We sit down and scoot close together, just like when we were kids.

Ever since I was a little girl, Jacob and I have sat together to watch the rain. Sometimes, when I was small, he'd push me into the mud and then Mama would tan his backside for it, but mostly we just sit quietly together, listening and watching it fall.

"Another year older," Jacob says, pulling a tin of cigarettes from the chest pocket of his shirt. He takes two and lights both up before handing one to me. "You feel any different?"

"Not a bit," I say, then take a drag from the cigarette. I blow the white-gray smoke out slow.

"You remember my nineteenth?" Jacob asks with a laugh.

I laugh, too. "Sure do. Can't forget somethin' like that."

"I don't even know how I found my way home. Most of that night is still hazy."

"I thought the broken nose would be reminder enough," I say, jostling him roughly in the shoulder. His nose still has a quirk in it from the break. We found out later that he'd not gotten into a fight, like we thought, but had fallen from a barstool drunk outta his damn mind, and the floor didn't catch him too kindly.

"Shit," he mumbles, rubbing his fingers across his nose. "That hurt like hell."

We lapse into silence. A heaviness settles across my shoulders as I watch the rain create puddles in the dirt, turning the hardpacked earth into mud that'll stick around for days.

"What now?" I ask.

"Hmm?"

"What are we supposed to be doin' with our lives? You're older than I am—shouldn't you be married with babies by now?"

"I could say the same for you."

"I prefer horses." I lean back and tip my face up as Jacob laughs.

"The life of a spinster, then?"

"Mama would die of a broken heart."

Jacob laughs a bit harder, but he doesn't disagree. I think about what Mama said in the kitchen, and her words bring me a bit of peace. But the question remains: What am I supposed to be doing with my life? Shouldn't I know by now?

We finish our cigarettes nice and slow. When we're done, Jacob pulls me in for a hug. I tuck myself into the spot beneath his chin and he kisses me atop the head. "Happy birthday, sis."

"Daisy!" Mama's voice calls from the house. "Come in here!" Jacob and I get up and walk back inside.

Mama's sitting in a chair with a knitted blanket spread out over her lap. Her fingers move quickly as she patches holes in the yarn in preparation for winter. I've never met a person, man nor woman, who's as prepared as Mama. She starts readying for winter on the first day of spring, and it's because of her that we never go hungry, are never without firewood or water during the long, cold months.

"Your father and I have a gift for you," Mama says. Her blue eyes land on Papa, and he shifts in his chair with a grunt.

"Sit down," he tells me, gesturing to the rocking chair across from him. I take a seat, then glance between my parents. Presents are a rarity around here, on account of money and the fact that I've got everything I could ever want.

Papa reaches into his back pocket and pulls out a sheathed knife. He hands it over to me, and I wrap my fingers around the hilt and pull the knife free.

The blade glints in the firelight, and I admire the fine work as I turn it from side to side. On closer inspection, I see my initials carved into the dark wood hilt.

"It's beautiful," I say softly. The blade is polished so clean that I can see my fractured reflection staring back at me.

"You like it?" Mama asks.

"I love it. Thank you." I stand and pull Papa in for a hug, and he smells like smoke and leather. Then I pull Mama in, and she kisses me on the forehead before I lean away.

"Why don't you play for us?" Mama asks.

"Sure." I buckle the new sheath around my waist before I walk down the hallway to the back bedroom.

My room is small, only big enough for a single bed, dresser, and desk that's cluttered with pencils and sketches. The window is open and the thin drapes Mama sewed for me dance in the damp breeze.

I grab my fiddle from under the bed and tighten up the bow as I walk back to where my family waits by the fire. The flames dance, tossing light and shadow across the walls. Jacob is reclining in his chair, his boots up on the hearth. His eyes are closed, but I can tell he's listening as I slip my fiddle into the spot between my shoulder and chin and start to play.

Mama smiles and nods her head slowly, and Papa's eyes get distant as he stares into the fire. I've been playing the fiddle since I was a kid, though I'm not sure they liked my music much back then. Papa taught me, and he used to play the guitar, too, but he don't pull it out anymore, not since his knuckles got stiff and painful.

One of Jacob's feet moves to the rhythm of my music, and I play for them until Papa dozes off.

Despite my full day of doing nothing, I feel sleep tugging

at my eyelids. Mama's big meals always do this to me—they're so good that I stuff myself too full and then fall right asleep.

I tell Mama and Jacob goodnight and give Papa a kiss on the cheek. After putting my fiddle away, I step outside into the moist air and take a deep breath. The rain has finally let up, but the ground has turned to mud, and everything smells rich and delicious. The moon is full and beautiful tonight, so I don't need a lantern to find my way to the outhouse. When I'm done, I step out and let the door fall closed behind me. In the distance, the singing of coyotes and crickets is drowned out by the sound of hooves rumbling over the wet plains.

My heartbeat quickens. It's not common to get many visitors through here. We live a mile from the main road, so anyone coming this way is certainly headed toward us and not just passing through.

I hurry to the house, my boots squelching in the mud, and then run inside without bothering to take them off.

"Mama! Papa!" Papa is still dozing by the fire and Mama is tidying up in the kitchen. She turns to look at me, rag in hand.

"What is it?"

"Horses coming down the road," I say. This gets Papa's attention, and he shoots up out of his chair and goes to the window. He stands there for a moment, his eyes squinted in the firelight, and the look on his grizzled face makes my stomach sink like a stone. He puts on his hat and yells for Jacob. I step out of the way as Papa hurries past me into his and Mama's bedroom. When he comes back out, he's carrying a shotgun.

"Jacob!" Papa yells again. "Get down here, son!"

"John?" Mama says, reaching for Papa as he hurries past. "John, what's going on?"

"Men comin' down the road," Papa says, "and I ain't expectin' no visitors." His eyes land on me. "Daisy, get down in the cellar. Hurry, now."

"No," I say defiantly. "I wanna help you."

"Don't back talk me," Papa says gruffly. "You get down in that cellar and you stay there. You hear me?"

I nod.

"You hear me?" Papa asks again, louder this time.

"Yes, sir."

"Then go!"

The root cellar is buried below the house, and there's a door built into the kitchen floor that Mama lifts and holds up for me. I hurry down the ladder and look back up at her.

"Mama, come on!" I urge, but she shakes her head. Her hands are shaking, but her expression is stern. "Mama, *please*," I beg.

"Lock the door," she says. "And keep quiet." She drops the door closed and sweeps a rug over it. The darkness swallows me. Fingers shaking, I fumble for the lock, finally getting it slid into place.

There's one small crack in the door overhead that the rug doesn't cover, and I stand up on my tiptoes to try to see what's happening. I can barely make out Mama's feet and her skirt swishing across the floor above me. Jacob's boots stomp through the house and the screen door creaks open. I'm breathing hard and my skin prickles with goose bumps in the damp, cool air.

Men's voices rumble, but I can't tell what they're saying. Then there's laughter, and more voices. Friends of Papa's, perhaps?

Boots shake the floorboards overhead and I shrink back, making myself small on the dirt floor.

"Margaret," says an unfamiliar voice. "It's right nice to see you."

"You as well, Cornelius."

"Please, call me Hopkins."

Hopkins, Hopkins. The name is familiar, but I ain't sure why. I know I've seen it somewhere recently. But where?

"Sit," Mama says. Chairs pull out from the table, the legs screeching across the floor.

"To what do we owe the pleasure?" Papa asks.

"Pleasure?" Hopkins laughs, and the sound of it is heavy and slow. "Ain't no pleasure in seein' me, I'm sure."

A long, full silence fills the air.

"Water?" Mama offers, and I let out the breath I was holding. The cups clunk onto the kitchen table, then there's the slosh of men drinking deeply. I can't see how many there are, but the feet coming through the house sounded like a cattle drive.

"Why've you come?" Papa's voice is tense, all formality gone.

Hopkins sighs, and the kitchen chair squeaks under his weight. "You know why I'm here, John."

Another silence, pulled tight, like a thread about to snap.

"Who told you?"

"Bastard who sold us both out," Hopkins says, his voice barely above a whisper. "Merriweather."

Now that name I know. Papa went to work at the Merriweather Mining Company after he returned home from the war. Weren't but a few years ago he left the mining business, and we've been growing corn and potatoes ever since.

"My family ain't got nothin' to do with this. Let's you and I step outside—handle this like men." The chair squeaks back as Papa stands.

"No," Jacob says, and I jump at the sound of the shotgun cocking. I dig my nails into my palms and bite my lip. Fabric and leather rustle as guns pull from holsters and hammers click into place.

"Jacob," Papa warns. "Put down the gun."

"Not until they leave," Jacob growls.

"I didn't come for you, son," Hopkins says. "Now get that muzzle outta my face 'fore you do somethin' stupid."

"Jacob," Mama says. "Listen to your father." Her voice is airy, the way it gets when she's trying not to cry.

"John," Hopkins says, a warning tone in his voice.

"Jacob, put the—"

A gunshot explodes through the house. Mama screams, and a body falls to the floor.

The first shot sets off a series of gunfire. A bullet rips through the floor overhead, splintering the wood before it embeds in the soft dirt at my feet. I scramble away, press myself against the cellar wall, try not to scream.

It's over in a matter of seconds. Blood drips through the floorboards overhead as heavy footsteps cross the kitchen. My ears ring, the sound of gunshots still echoing in my head.

"You stupid boy," Hopkins says. "Didn't have to end this way."

"Go . . . to . . . hell," Jacob wheezes, his voice wet, fading.

"At least it'll be warm."

A hammer clicks, and one final shot is fired.

I close my eyes. The silence settles over me like snow on our fields in early November. Jacob smiles, packs a snowball. I ride Lucky bareback, let the wind sting my face as I tip my head to the sky.

"Burn it down," says Hopkins. "And let's get the hell out of here."

I've gone numb, the ringing in my ears drowning out my thoughts. I don't want to think, don't want to feel. If only I could close my eyes and not have to open them again.

I don't move. Not until the smell of smoke reaches me.

Legs trembling, I push to my feet and reach for the lock on the door overhead. My hands shake so hard I can't hold the lock steady enough to release it.

"Shit," I mumble, then immediately regret it. Mama doesn't like when I talk like that.

The lock finally comes loose, and I push the door with all

my might. I struggle up the ladder and climb into the kitchen. What I see forces a strained cry to tear from my chest.

Mama's lifeless on the floor, her face a bloody, broken mess. The wall behind her is splattered with brain and blood.

"Mama," I whisper. "Mama, please." I crawl to her, my hands and knees slipping in the blood pooled around her. "Mama, no, please, *please*." I cradle what's left of her head in my lap, but no matter how I beg or scream or cry, she doesn't return to me.

Across the kitchen lie Papa and Jacob. Jacob's face is turned in my direction, his lips spattered with blood and his forehead blasted through with a single bullet. Multiple gunshot wounds litter his chest, and his blue eyes are open, glassy, unseeing.

I can't see Papa's face—he's tangled up in an overturned chair, blood pooling around him.

He's dead—they're all dead.

Smoke thickens overhead and I begin to cough. Heat bites at my bare arms and sweat has broken out across my forehead. I've gotta get them out of here.

I stand and loop my hands under Mama's arms. Grunting, I attempt to pull her across the kitchen floor. She moves but an inch before I have to catch my breath. She's heavier than I thought, and my trembling hands can't seem to get a good hold on her. My eyes burn, and my lungs are on fire. I can't even see through the kitchen into the living room through the thick white smoke.

I don't want to leave Mama here, I *can't* leave her here. With all the strength left in me, I struggle to my feet, then take hold of her arms and pull. Inch by inch, I drag her across the kitchen to the tiny door that leads out the back. I'm screaming and crying as I finally drag her down the porch steps. My boots slip in the mud, but I don't stop. I growl and yell and fight as hard as I can to drag Mama a safe distance from the house.

I run back up the steps and yank open the screen door,

but I'm too late. The fire is spreading fast, and beams of timber creak and splinter overhead. I move to step into the kitchen, try to fight through the smoke and the heat, but I can't. A window beside me explodes, scattering shards of glass as I scream.

"Papa! Jacob!"

I want to go to them, to drag their bodies from the flames.

Coughing and sobbing, I stumble down the steps into the yard. My knees finally give way and I fall in the mud beside Mama.

The fire hisses as it burns, and I watch through teary eyes as it grows to swallow up what remains of the house.

And there's not a damn thing I can do.

CHAPTER 2
August 1880

DON'T TAKE LONG for townsfolk to arrive. The sheriff and his deputies are first. They try to ask me questions, but the only word I can mumble is "Hopkins." Then the wagons roll up, filled with the men and women I've known most of my life. I can't bear to look at them—can't handle the horrified looks on their faces. Billy's here, along with his parents and sister. Jacob was his best friend—has been since they were boys. He don't cry, but I can tell he wants to.

Nice ladies try to take me home. They want to get me cleaned up, feed me, give me a soft place to put my head. But I don't want any of those things. I want to stay right here, where I belong.

Some of the men try to take Mama's body away, but I pull out my knife and scream until they back far, far away. Even Billy don't approach me after that.

The night slips away, and I'm the only one left when the house has burned to the ground, diminished to nothing but fallen beams and smoking rubble.

I look up at the sky and it's a perfect summer blue. It's gonna be a hot one, the type of day that made Papa pull his hat low over his eyes and made Jacob strip off his shirt. Oh, how the girls in town love that.

I push to my feet. My hands shake and my knees wobble, but I don't fall. Instead, I stalk to the barn and grab a shovel.

I whisper to myself as I work. "Hopkins."

I think of his gravelly voice while I dig Mama's grave. "Hopkins."

I wonder what it would be like to put a bullet between his eyes while I nail three wooden crosses together using old wood from the barn. "Hopkins."

It takes me all day. The townsfolk would've helped if I hadn't sent them off, Billy would've helped, but I want to do this alone. I *need* to do this alone.

My hands are blistered and bleeding as I lower Mama into the grave. She falls, without grace, into the hole, her body twisted at strange angles. The sight is so obscene that I'm filled with disgust and shame.

Tears stream down my cheeks as I start to fill the hole. The dirt makes soft sounds as it falls across her chest, her arms, her slender fingers.

I find Papa's and Jacob's bones buried in the ash, and they're waxy and brittle as I place them in their own graves.

And when it's done, when the people I love most are buried side by side, I let out a long breath and pray to die. How much easier that would be than to go on living without them.

Smoke from the smoldering rubble still curls up, up, and into the evening sky. I turn and look back at what's left of the house. There ain't much—just ash and death and ghosts of what it used to be. I take a steadying breath and go in search of anything salvageable.

My clothes, my sketchbook, my fiddle: all burned up. Mama's handmade quilts: gone. Papa's old guitar: gone. Jacob's collection of feathers: gone. The beams that held up the house, the strength that held this family together, have crumbled and fallen.

I find Mama's cookware, her cast-iron pans. I think of all the corn bread she baked, the coffee she brewed, right here in our little kitchen.

I won't ever be able to get that picture out of my head: Mama's brain on the kitchen wall, her blood staining the floorboards. The thought brings tears to my eyes, and I wipe them away with a rough hand.

In what used to be Mama and Papa's room, I find an old steel lockbox Papa kept under the bed. The box is warped, and it takes a heavy hand to force it open. When the lid comes loose, I find Papa's old revolver inside.

With shaking hands, I lift the revolver from the box. It sits cradled in my palms, the metal gleaming in the sunset light. I take it in one hand. With a squeeze of the trigger, all of this could be over. The thought brings me peace.

Before I can change my mind, I lift the gun to my head and pull the trigger.

CHAPTER 3
August 1880

NOTHING HAPPENS—GUN ain't even loaded, for fuck's sake.

I drop the revolver and a puff of ash rises into the evening breeze. I let out a shuddering breath, then hold up a hand and find it trembling.

I spend the night in the barn with Lucky and my old mare Sassy—it's the only place left in this world that feels like home. I don't sleep well, and only in fits and starts. My eyes are swollen and raw from crying, and when I wake in the morning I feel the dampness of tears on my cheeks. In my dreams I watched Mama die, and I awaken with such a strong urge to hold her that my body aches.

I stumble out into the sun, my head pounding and my stomach churning with bile.

Seeing the graves reminds me of the hell that's become my life. In an early-morning daze I could've sworn I'd dreamed it all, but now I know it's real—painfully real. The three crosses I nailed together look feeble in the pale morning light. They're small and slightly crooked and don't do the people buried beneath them any justice. I can't stand to look at them.

I brush the dirt from Lucky's coat before saddling him up. I put Sassy's halter on and hold the lead rope while I struggle into the saddle. I've never felt so weak, not even when Lucky threw me when I was young and bruised my ribs so bad I could barely breathe for days. Mama nursed me back to health, her hands gentle as she rubbed salve on my chest and spoon-fed me since I couldn't sit up. Thinking of it now should bring a smile to my face, but my lips are so dry and cracked that I can't even muster that without pain.

"Get on," I say to Lucky, then cluck my tongue and he starts to walk. Sassy walks beside us, her head bobbing and her ears flicking back and forth. Gentlest horse I've ever met, this old mare. I reach over and scratch her between the ears. It makes my stomach twist thinking of what I have to do.

The sun creeps across the summer sky as I ride down the long, dusty road into town. I pass a wagon and some riders along the way, and they look at me sideways. I must look about as bad as I feel.

When I get to town, I hitch Sassy and Lucky up to the post outside the sheriff's office. I head inside and Sheriff Giddons looks up from his desk. He stands and removes his hat.

"Miss Allen, please, sit." He pulls a wobbly wooden chair out from the corner and sets me down in it. He fills a cup of water from a bucket and hands it to me. I sip it slowly, savoring every drop.

"Are you okay—you hurt?" He seems to want to reach out, touch me, but thinks better of it. "I didn't get a good look at you. You wouldn't let no one get close enough to make sure you was all right."

"I'm fine," I say softly, and tip the rest of the water into my mouth.

"Gimme some," mumbles the town drunk, who's locked in a cell in the corner. "I'm thirsty too, Sheriff!"

"You shut your mouth," the sheriff snaps at him. "I'm tryin' to have a goddamn conversation over here."

I sigh, and Sheriff Giddons turns back around.

"Jesus, I'm so sorry," he says, his voice quiet. "I just can't wrap my head around it." He sits on the edge of his desk and folds his arms. The star on his chest is polished to a shine. A lot of good it did, that star.

"It was a man named Hopkins," I say. "You know anything about him?"

"Not personally, no. But he's in the paper enough." He grabs a newspaper from his desk and hands it to me. The article, about a murder and kidnapping up in Golden, is familiar, and now I remember where I saw Hopkins's name before. Papa was reading the story just a few days ago, his eyes troubled as he rocked in his chair and turned the pages with quiet focus.

"Papa knew him," I say softly.

"How?"

"Don't know. Never spoke of him before, but they knew each other. Somethin' to do with the Merriweather mine."

"In Pueblo?"

"Just south of there." I look down at my hands, trace the lines of dirt etched into my palms. "Are ya gonna do anything?"

The sheriff lets out a long, heavy sigh. "I sent some men after 'em, soon as we saw what they did to your folks. Sons of bitches killed one of my best deputies, God rest his soul." He takes off his hat and holds it to his chest.

So that's it, then. Sheriff ain't gonna do anything else about it. If it were his family buried six under, then would he try harder?

Don't matter, I think. *What's done is done.*

"Your daughter still wanna learn to ride?" I ask.

Sheriff Giddons quirks a bushy brow at me. "Why?"

"I've got Sassy outside. Remember her?"

"Of course. What're ya sayin'?"

"I've changed my mind about sellin'."

Sheriff Giddons gets a sad look in his eyes, but he gives me a firm nod. "Let's take a look."

We walk outside together. Sassy and Lucky are hitched at the post, nuzzling each other affectionately. Sassy is smaller than Lucky, a good size for a girl to grow into. I tell the sheriff this and he nods.

"You sure you wanna do this?" he asks. "You don't gotta. Take a few days and think about it."

Of course I don't, but I've got no choice. I don't got a dollar to my name. I couldn't even buy a bullet to kill myself with.

"I'm sure."

He sighs, scratches his chin. "How much you want for her?"

"Ten."

The sheriff smooths out his mustache, then reaches into his pocket and pulls out fifteen dollars.

I take the money with a nod, then step off the porch to Sassy. I bury my face in her neck and take a deep breath. I've always loved the way she smells, like hay and dirt and my childhood. Whenever I used to get angry at Mama or after I'd had a fight with Jacob, I'd run out to the stable and stand like this with Sassy until I'd stopped crying.

"Be good for that little girl," I whisper to her. And then to the sheriff, "Take care of her."

"We will. And we'd take care of you, too, if you'd let us."

"I don't need no one to take care of me," I mumble, running my hand over Sassy's soft coat.

"You can't live out there all by yourself," he says.

Before I can change my mind, I give Sassy a final kiss and lead Lucky away. I don't turn around, not even when Sassy whinnies out in alarm, wondering why she's not coming with us. The sheriff calls my name, but I don't respond.

CHAPTER 4
August 1880

I FIND SOLACE in a whiskey bottle. Mr. Ebb Schilling, the man who owns the saloon, gives it to me for free, and I ain't about to let it go to waste.

I sit on Jacob's favorite barstool, the one with his initials carved into it, and drink straight outta the bottle. Mr. Schilling leans his elbows on the bar and gives me a sad look.

"Don't look at me like that," I mumble.

"How am I lookin' at ya?"

"Like you feel bad for me."

"Well I do, Daisy. We all do." He gestures around the saloon, at the few people drinking here, and they quickly turn their eyes away.

"Waste of time," I mumble.

Mr. Schilling ignores my comment. He runs a hand over his long mustache and sighs. "What're ya gonna do about a service?"

"A service?" I pause mid-drink and look up at him.

"Your folks deserve somethin' nice. Your brother, too."

"No," I say, and then take another drink. It burns like hell and I grit my teeth against it. "No service."

"Why?" he asks. "Don't seem right not to do somethin' for 'em."

I imagine a service. People crying, dressed in black, sweltering under the summer sun. Would they wanna dig Mama up, bury her in a proper coffin?

"No service," I say again, and when Mr. Schilling starts to protest, I grab my bottle of whiskey and leave him standing at the bar alone.

Back outside, I wander along the boardwalk and tip back the bottle for another drink. The thoroughfare is quiet, with only a few people coming and going, and they look at me with a mixture of discomfort and pity.

Maybe they wanna come say something, offer their condolences. Maybe they don't know how, or don't know what to say. They hesitate, pause, then move on when they see the whiskey in my hand.

I keep on walking, and it ain't until I get to The Dusty Rose, the whorehouse, that anyone stops for a word.

"Daisy, oh honey, come here." It's Clementine, a young woman who showed up in Rock Creek a couple years ago, come with nothing but a bag and a past she wasn't keen to talk about. I'm sure her name ain't really Clementine, but she wouldn't tell me even if I asked.

She pulls me in for a hug, and her hair is soft and smells of honeysuckle as it brushes my cheek. "Come on, sit down, let me have a look at you." She pulls me over to a bench in the shade and sits down beside me. "I just . . . I don't even know what to say, 'cept for I'm so sorry."

"Ain't nothin' for you to be sorry about." I take a sip of whiskey, then offer it to her. She accepts it and takes a long drink, then clears her throat and hands it back.

"You wanna talk about it?" she asks.

"No." I shrug, looking away. It's a constant fight to keep my face neutral and not let myself cry like a damn child. I already did enough crying, and here's not the place.

"How's about a bath, then? You look like you could use one." She bumps me playfully, and the insult brings a hint of a smile to my lips, though it don't last long.

"Okay."

She leads me inside, where other girls are lounging on sofas, fanning themselves to keep cool in the heat. I'm greeted with a harmony of voices telling me how sorry they are, offering me their thoughts and prayers, telling me it'll be okay. I don't believe them, but I appreciate their sentiments.

The madam of the house, Elma Hewitt, looks down on us from the second-floor balcony. Her brown hair is piled up on top of her head and she wears a dress in dark plum with lace up to her chin.

"I offered her a bath," Clementine tells her. "Seems the least we can do."

Elma descends the stairs, the skirt of her dress trailing behind her. I ain't sure what to expect, but she surprises me when she pulls a tin of finely rolled cigarettes out of her cleavage and offers me one. I take it and put it between my lips, and she lights it for me with a match.

"Go on," she says, her voice low and soft.

Clementine leads me away, smoke from my cigarette curling behind us. The bathing room is down a hallway behind a door with roses painted on it. Clementine pushes the door open, then offers to help me with my bath.

"I can wash myself just fine, thanks."

"If you change your mind, just holler." She hands me a towel and a bar of soap, then leaves me alone with the gentle click of the door.

I put the bottle of whiskey down, then strip out of my clothes. Everything hurts. My head, my body, my heart. My skin is coated in ash and dust, my hair a mess of tangles.

There's a mirror on the wall across from me, but I don't look in it.

I slip into the water slowly, and even though it ain't but lukewarm, it still feels damn good.

Whiskey in one hand, smoking cigarette in the other, I recline in the metal tub and let out a long, heavy sigh. The water darkens as it lifts the filth from my skin.

I can hear the ladies in the parlor talking, and I wonder if they know how their voices carry.

They're talking about what a pity it is, what a terrible thing that happened. They start talking about my brother, and his name is sweet on their tongues.

I wonder how many of these ladies he's laid with. His pale hair, blue eyes, and easy smile kept his hands full with hungry women. I suppose they'll miss him now, too. We all will.

I take a heavy drag on the cigarette and it makes me cough. The cough shakes my resolve, turns into tears. I start to cry, trying to mask the sound so the whores can't hear me. It shakes my chest, steals my breath, and I cover my mouth with a hand to muffle the sobs.

I realize, with painful clarity, that no amount of whiskey or fine cigarettes will ever dull the pain.

The sunset paints the sky the color of flames—the color of death. I watch the sun go down from the roof of the barn and wonder if I'll ever look at a sunset the same way again.

The town held a service for that deputy who was killed chasing after Hopkins and his men, but I didn't go. I should have—Mama would've wanted me to—but I didn't. Couldn't stomach the thought of it.

The days are passing by in a haze of whiskey and grief. I ain't even sure what day it is, or how long it's been since I slept last. All I know is what's left of the house has finally stopped smoldering, and whatever cleanliness I had after my bath at The Dusty Rose is long gone.

Nice ladies from town keep coming to visit me, carrying baskets of baked goods with them. They bring pies, loaves of bread, flowers to leave on the graves. I eat what I can, but my stomach's so sour with whiskey that half of it always comes back up. Clementine stopped by too, brought me a tin of cigarettes, and I'm chain-smoking as darkness falls.

The stars come to life one by one, and I remember the stories Papa used to tell about the creatures in the sky. He'd show me how to connect the stars, make pictures out of them, and we'd lie on our backs in the field and talk for hours. Mama always had to come out and find us and bring us home for supper, and I'd tell her our stories on the way back.

I take a drag from the cigarette and flick the ash away forcefully, then grab the bottle from beside me and take a long drink. It's near tasteless now—probably burned my throat so bad I can't even tell how terrible it is. But it don't matter. Nothing does anymore.

I'm half-asleep when something stirs me awake. It's the sound of hooves on dirt, a horse snorting. I'm taken back to that night, the herd coming down the road, the men and their voices muffled by the floorboards overhead.

I grab Papa's gun from the rooftop beside me and aim it into the dark.

"Who's there?" I yell, still blinking sleep from my eyes.

"Whoa, easy," says a man's voice. "It's me. Billy."

Billy. He ain't come around since the fire. His mama said he went off somewhere, needed to clear his head. I didn't think I cared, but now I know it ain't true.

"I'm comin' up." He climbs into our old wagon, then reaches for the barn roof as I put Papa's gun down. As soon as he's over the edge, I grab him and pull him toward me.

"Daisy," he whispers, but I kiss his words away.

The summer night is all around us. I can't get him

undressed fast enough, can't feel enough of him against my skin.

His lips are on my jaw, my neck. He lays me down and presses his chest to mine, and I wish the weight of him could smother all this grief that threatens to pull me down. I'd rather drown in him than in a bottle of cheap whiskey.

He takes me under the summer stars. His breath is heavy in my ear, and it hitches as I dig my fingernails into his back, pulling him closer, closer. This time ain't like the others. This time, I *need* him.

He braces himself on the roof with one hand, and the other he tangles in my hair. I tip my head back and his mouth finds my neck, and then it's on my lips. The kiss is soft, sweet, until it turns salty with tears.

Billy pulls away and brushes a thumb across my cheek. "Daisy," he says again, but I shake my head.

"Just kiss me," I whisper, and he does.

He helps me into my clothes when we're done, and I light up a cigarette as we sit together beneath the stars. We take turns smoking and drinking from the whiskey bottle until not a drop remains.

"I should've married you," I say. "Mama liked you."

"I know."

"We could've built a house. Had kids. Died old and unafraid." Tears well up in my eyes. "Mama would've been happy."

"I know." He pulls me in, wraps his arms around me. His lips are in my hair, at my temple, on my cheek. The tears shake my chest, knock the air out of me. But Billy doesn't let go.

We fall asleep tangled up in one another, and I don't open my eyes until the early hours of the morning. It's almost dawn, and the sun will soon come up over the hills in the distance, waking the birds so they sing in the trees.

I sit up slowly, careful not to wake Billy. My mouth tastes of whiskey and smoke and tears. It's a taste I've become all too familiar with.

The sun is slowly creeping toward the horizon, and I believe it's playing tricks on me, because I swear I see my brother standing at the foot of his own grave.

"Jacob?" I whisper. He looks up at me, but his face ain't right. It's too square, too sharp, too *wrong*.

The man, whoever he is, backs away from the graves. A pale palomino waits for him by the road, and he's into the saddle and gone before I can think of what to say.

My days are all the same now. I drink at the saloon until Mr. Schilling kicks me out, and then I hang around the girls at The Dusty Rose until Madam Elma tells me I'm scaring her customers away. Some nights I lie with Billy, hoping he'll fill the emptiness I carry around, but I never stay full for long.

I'm sitting by myself at the saloon, thinking about the best way to off myself, when the swinging doors creak open behind me. I don't bother to turn around. It's evening and those doors have been swinging all night. The saloon's full of men just finished with a day's work, and they're thirsty and looking for a way to blow off steam. Half of them will walk down to The Dusty Rose when they're done here, and the other half will go home to their wives—probably.

A man steps up beside me, too close for comfort, and I tighten the hold on my whiskey glass.

"Beer," he says, and Mr. Schilling goes about pouring him a glass. His voice ain't familiar, which is what makes me turn.

He looks so much like Jacob that it feels like a rusty knife's gone through my heart. Blond hair, eyes like the sky, and a face the girls must go crazy for. But he ain't Jacob—I can see that clearly now.

I grab the knife from my hip and have it at the man's neck before he can blink. "You," I growl, pressing it into the soft skin at the base of his throat. "Who are you, and what the hell do you want with me?"

The saloon's gone still. No one moves to stop me.

"You the Allen girl?" he asks.

"You the fool who was creepin' around my property?"

He hesitates before answering. "What'll it take to get you to lower that knife?"

"The *truth*."

"Then yes," he says. "But I ain't gonna tell you why less you lower that knife."

My hand shakes. It'd be easy to twist my wrist, send the polished blade through his throat. But those eyes—like Jacob's, like Mama's.

I lower the knife and fall back onto Jacob's favorite barstool. Everyone in the saloon seems to let out a collective breath.

"Forgive her brashness," Mr. Schilling says as he slides the beer glass across the bar. "She's just lost her family."

"Shut it, Schilling," I growl. "That ain't no stranger's business."

"Was it Hopkins killed 'em?" the stranger asks.

I freeze. Others in the saloon go quiet.

"What the hell you know about Hopkins?"

The stranger tips his beer back and finishes it in a few big gulps. Then he wipes his mouth and smiles.

"Eat supper with me, and I'll tell ya."

CHAPTER 5
August 1880

H E BUYS ME supper at old lady Loretta's down the road. It's quiet, as most of the working men have already finished their food and are off to find whiskey and women.

Loretta's restaurant has been here for years—ever since I was a kid. Businesses have come and gone over the years, people die or move away, but Loretta's always stays put.

She serves us what she's got left of her baked potatoes and flaky biscuits. My stomach growls and pinches, and it's a struggle not to stuff my face. If I do, I'll be out back in a minute chucking it all back up.

The man watches me while I eat, and I ain't sure I like the way his eyes study me.

"So," I say, wiping my mouth with a napkin after I've swallowed my potatoes. "What do you want?"

"To know about that fire, and what happened beforehand."

I take a sip of coffee and narrow my eyes. "What's it matter to you?"

Loretta brings us a plate with a single piece of pie on it, and the stranger leans forward with his fork.

"Not for you," she says, waving him off. "For you, Daisy." Her voice is soft as she slides the plate across the table to me. She places one of her old hands on mine and gives it a soft squeeze. "If you need anything, dear, you know I'm always here."

"Thanks, Loretta." I smile up at her until she walks away, then pull the pie closer. It's raspberry, and the flavor is so strong and full that it makes my mouth pucker.

"I'm here to find out more about Hopkins," the man says.

"He's a murderous son of a bitch," I growl. "Killed my family, burned my house down. And now here we are." I hold up my hands. "Ain't it fuckin' grand?"

"Are you still drunk?" he asks.

"Probably." I take another sip of coffee and use a finger to wipe up the last of the raspberry smeared across the plate.

"Why your family? Why not terrorize the town instead?"

I lean back in the chair, which squeaks under my weight. "He knew my papa, sounded like. And a man called Merriweather. They worked together."

"Where?"

"The mines, years ago."

"So why'd he come back now?"

I shrug and pull my knife from the sheath at my hip. The man eyes it warily.

"I need to know more," he says, leaning forward. "I wanna know who he was with, how many there were, what they were sayin'—"

"Why the hell do you care? What's it matter who he had with him? It's all done now. He's probably halfway to Cali-fuckin'-fornia by now."

"You ain't the only person he's hurt," the man says. He sits back from the table, his blue eyes gone dark. "He took someone, and we're trackin' him down."

My heart thumps once—hard.

We're trackin' him down.

I'd never thought to track him, not just because I ain't any good at tracking, but because I never realized that was an option. I've thought about what it would feel like to see Hopkins, to hold the barrel of Papa's revolver up to his head, but I never took it seriously. But this . . . this could mean getting revenge for what he did to my family.

"I wanna go with you."

At first the man looks surprised, then humored.

"You don't even know who I am."

I hold out my hand. "Daisy Allen." Then, with a smirk, "But you knew that already."

After a moment of deliberation, the man puts his hand in mine and gives it a rough shake. "Henry McCloud. But you still ain't comin'."

"Like hell I ain't. If you're goin' after that bastard, then so am I."

"You'd leave this place?" He waves a hand to gesture around us. "Why?"

" 'Cause I can't stand to look at those goddamn crosses anymore." My fingers curl into a fist and I slam it down on the table, making the coffee in our cups spill. "There ain't nothin' left for me here. If I've got a chance in hell to kill that bastard, then I'm gonna take it."

"And what'll happen while you're gone? You'd leave that property?"

"It'll be waitin' for her when she gets back," Loretta says, coming over from where she's been eavesdropping at the other side of the restaurant. She puts a hand on my shoulder and gives it a squeeze. "We'll take care of things here. You go get that man, and make sure he suffers for what he's done." Her eyes have gone glassy, and she lifts a wrinkled hand to wipe away the tears before they can fall.

I'm not the only person the Hopkins gang hurt. They killed that deputy, too, and his family is mourning just like I am. Mama and Papa had friends in this town, people who loved them. And Jacob had his fellas, not to mention the girls with their pink cheeks and quick laughter. Of the four of us, I'd be the least missed. How wrong it is that I'm the only one left.

"Well?" I narrow my eyes and study Henry's face. He's grizzled, dirty, has a hint of a pale beard. His skin is browned from the summer sun, his nails packed with dirt. But he's got fire in his eyes—the angry kind. And when he lets out a tense sigh, I smile.

"Fine. But I ain't sure the others are gonna like this . . ."

My goodbyes are brief and few. Loretta gives me a strong hug, promises to care for my property while I'm away. I know she will, along with the other folks of Rock Creek. We may be simple, but we're loyal.

I think to go by Billy's house, hug him one last time, but I think better of it. Seeing his face wouldn't do me any good now. He'd make me weak, and that's something I can't afford to be.

We stop by The Dusty Rose on the way out of town, but it's busy tonight and Clementine ain't standing outside like she usually is. Another girl waits in her place, leaning up against a wooden beam, her face illuminated by lantern light. She smiles at Henry, fans herself demurely, and nods toward the brothel, but he shakes his head. She looks disappointed as her eyes turn to me.

"I'm lookin' for Clementine," I say.

"She's occupied," the girl answers.

"Can you give her a message?"

"Sure. For twenty-five cents." She holds out a hand and I clench my jaw.

"Twenty-five cents? You gotta be kiddin—"

"Here." Henry flips a coin her way and she catches it easily.

"Much obliged." She tucks it into a discreet pocket at her hip and smiles at me. "Well?"

"Tell her I'm goin' after Hopkins. Ain't sure when I'll be back. Ask her to tell Billy goodbye for me. And thank her . . . for everything."

The girl nods. "I'll tell her."

Before riding away, I turn to look back at Rock Creek.

The moon is high, painting the buildings in pale silver. Lantern light glows from windows and on boardwalks. Two men smoke cigarettes in the dark, a cat climbs on the apple crates stacked up outside Loretta's restaurant, and everything feels so much like home that my chest squeezes. But a mile off the main road, there's a house burned to ash, with three wooden crosses that weren't ever meant to be there.

I think about going home one last time, to say goodbye, but I can't. I've spent too long staring at those crosses, wishing there was a fourth one. But now I've got something to live for, something to die for. And the longer I linger here, the farther away Hopkins and his men move.

"Let's go," I tell Henry, then tip my hat low and turn Lucky toward the road.

CHAPTER 6
August 1880

WE RIDE OUT of Rock Creek together, our horses side by side. Henry ain't too talkative, which I'd typically appreciate, but I've got questions.

"Who's 'we'?"

"Eh?" He's digging in his pockets looking for something, not listening.

"You got travelin' companions?"

"You could say that. We're more like family than companions, though."

Family. What I wouldn't give to have mine back.

"How many of you are there?" Henry takes a moment to reply, and I look over at him with a quirked brow. "Can't count that high?"

He lets out a surprised laugh. "Damn, woman. Ain't known me but an hour and you're already makin' jokes." He finds what he's looking for—a tin of cigarettes—and offers me one.

"Thanks." I accept it after he's lit them up using a match

struck on the horn of his saddle. It tastes different than my usual cigarettes—rolled with his own tobacco—but I like the flavor. I take a few drags, let out a breath of smoke, and flick away the ash. "How far we gotta go?"

"Few miles outside of town." He looks over at me through the smoke. "We like to keep to our own."

"Then we've got somethin' in common."

We follow the dirt road for a mile or so, then cut off and head into the plains, passing through clusters of sagebrush with gnarled branches and silver-gray leaves. Coyotes scream in the distance, probably over a fresh kill. Their voices carry on the wind, causing Lucky to snort. He ain't never liked coyotes, or even rabbits for that matter. Big baby, this one.

Henry leads me down toward the river, where the grasses grow tall and plains cottonwoods line the banks. Mosquitos are heavy down here, and I'm swatting them away as wagons and a crackling fire come into view.

Everyone looks up as we ride into camp. There are more of them than I'd thought—quite a few more. An older woman, her face lit by firelight, stands up when she sees us.

"Who's this?" she asks. She has wrinkles around her eyes and her mouth, and her gaze is sharp.

"She's the one had her family killed by Hopkins," Henry explains. The woman's eyes soften as he swings down off his horse and motions for me to do the same.

I hesitate, taking a moment to scan the people around the fire, but Henry looks none too patient.

"Well come on then. You wanna see the boss or not?"

"Keep your pants on," I grumble. I finish off the last bit of my cigarette and then swing out of the saddle.

"This way." Henry leads me past the campfire, where two more women and one man sit staring into the flames. They look up at me as I pass, firelight and curiosity dancing in their eyes.

Cots and canvas lean-tos are scattered about, and there's a chuck wagon piled high with sacks of flour, beans, and boxes of dried apples. Looks like they plan to be on the road for a while.

We walk to the edge of camp, toward a tent that's bigger than the rest. There's a table and two chairs sitting outside, playing cards spread out haphazardly. Candles burn in lanterns hanging from the tent posts, and they toss firelight as they sway in the summer breeze. Three men stand in the darkness nearby smoking cigarettes and talking quietly.

"Who the hell is this?" one of them asks, his voice heavy with drink. He has an angry mouth and a long mustache that looks none too nice on his face.

"Get lost, Farley," Henry says. "This don't concern drunks."

"Say that again," Farley growls, stepping toward Henry.

"Mr. Farley," says the man in the middle, his voice low and serious. "We can continue our conversation later. Seems Mr. McCloud here has someone he'd like me to meet."

Farley spits at Henry's feet before pushing past us to go find a spot at the campfire. His eyes linger on me as he passes, and I stare at him right back.

"Apologies, miss," says the fella who broke up the argument. "He's a sour one." The man takes a drag on his cigarette and looks to Henry. "What's this all about?"

"She's from Rock Creek, the one I told you about. Says her family had a run-in with Hopkins."

"No, Hopkins killed them," I correct him. "And then he burned my house down."

"Goddamn—I'm sorry to hear that," the man says. "That Hopkins is a foul fucking bastard."

"I wanna kill him," I say, my fists tightening at my sides. It feels good to say it out loud.

The man laughs, then takes another drag and exhales a long stream of gray smoke into the night air. "Seems like you and I would get along just fine. What's your name?"

"Daisy. Daisy Allen." I hold out a hand and he gives it a firm shake.

"It's a pleasure to meet you. My name's William Steinburn, and this here is Patrick Carr." He motions to the man still standing next to him, who hasn't said a word. Carr tips his hat to me. "And it seems you've already met Mr. McCloud." He claps Henry on the shoulder and smiles. "We wondered what was keeping him so long."

"He bought me dinner." I nod my head in Henry's direction. "Just wanted answers outta me, but he tried to be a gentleman, at least."

"Oh?" Steinburn looks over at Henry. "Well, can't say that comes as a surprise. Women have been known to get Mr. McCloud right distracted. Ain't that right, son?"

Henry pulls his hat low and looks the other way.

"No matter," Steinburn continues. "So, Daisy, you know anything about this Hopkins? What he wanted, where he was headed?"

I shake my head. "All I know is he killed my family, and I ain't gonna rest until that bastard's in the ground."

Steinburn smiles. "So you're wanting to join us, then?"

"Yes, sir. And I won't be no burden on you. I can do whatever you need. I just want someplace to stay, and some people to travel with."

Steinburn goes silent for a long time, for such a long time that I start fiddling with my fingernails like Mama always told me not to.

"We don't have much to offer," he says finally. "Can't promise you we'll even find Hopkins in the end, but we'll do our damnedest. And you'd be expected to do your fair share of the work around here."

"I ain't no stranger to hard work," I say firmly. "I'll do what it takes to stay here."

Steinburn looks at Carr, who shrugs his shoulders in a lazy way. With a smile, Steinburn holds out a rugged hand. I take it and give him a firm shake.

"Let's kill the bastard together," he says, and I smile for what feels like the first time in a long time.

CHAPTER 7
August 1880

HENRY MAKES QUICK introductions, but there are too many names for me to remember, and it's not easy to make out faces by firelight. I don't much feel like talking, so I ask Henry to show me where I can sleep.

"Don't matter," he says. "Just don't sleep too close to Burns—he makes one hell of a stink."

"I heard that, ya shit," comes a grouchy voice from across camp. Henry tips his hat to me and then wanders off into the night, leaving me standing near the fire alone.

I'm about to find a place to lie down when the older woman I saw before comes walking toward me. She's got graying hair wound up in a tight bun and a burning cigarette in one hand.

"Thought you might need this," she says, tossing me the bedroll that was tucked under her arm. I catch it and smile.

"Thank you, ma'am."

"Name's Ethel." She holds out a hand and we shake.

"Daisy."

Ethel nods as she exhales a breath of smoke. "You'd best get some sleep. I'll have work enough for you tomorrow." She turns and walks away, her gait slow and heavy.

I lay out my bedroll in a grassy spot, then take off my hat and stretch out on the ground.

The stars are bright overhead, and I watch them twinkle as my eyelids get heavy.

Mama used to say that our loved ones are never truly gone, and that they're up in the stars watching down on us. I hope she was right. I search for the three brightest stars in the sky and reach up with my fingers as if to snatch the light from the inky blackness. How I wish I could carry those stars in my pocket and keep them beside me wherever I go. At least then I wouldn't feel so alone.

Tears roll slowly down my cheeks, and I brush them away before turning over to get some shut-eye.

The next morning comes on slow. I feel the sun on my face, warming my eyelids, but I keep them closed while I listen to the sounds around me.

The horses are eating nearby, and there's a smell of smoke in the air. The fire crackles softly, and voices murmur. Someone snores, someone else sighs. After being alone for so long, it feels strange to be surrounded by so much life.

I open my eyes and sit up with a grunt, the knot in my back popping as I twist and stretch. The sun is bright already, and I run a hand over my face before putting on my hat and pulling the brim low.

A few of the men I met last night—Steinburn, Carr, and that grouchy fella Farley—are standing at the edge of camp with their horses tacked up. Their shotguns gleam in the morning sun, strapped alongside the saddlebags and other cargo. Henry's with them, and Steinburn gives him a handshake before the three mount up and ride out. They trot past me, and Steinburn tips his hat. I watch them ride off into the distance, the horses' hooves kicking up dust as they go.

"Mornin'!" says a chipper voice behind me, and I turn to look up at the young woman. The sun's bright, so I've gotta squint to see her. She's got dark hair and brown skin, and her smile is quick and wide.

"Mornin'," I say, getting to my feet and dusting myself off. "Where are they gettin' off to?" I gesture in the direction the men went.

"Gotta pick some things up in town before we head out. I'm Alice, by the way," she says in a distinctly Spanish accent. She holds out a hand and I shake it.

"Daisy."

"Cookie's got some food ready over here, if you want some?"

She leads me to the chuck wagon, where a man is slopping food into chipped bowls. He's got a round face and kind eyes, and wears a stained apron around his middle.

"Mr. Burns," Alice says, "this is our new friend Daisy, and she's mighty hungry."

"Good to meet'cha, Daisy. You can call me Burns, or Cookie if you'd like. Here, eat up." He slides a bowl toward me and the oats almost spill over the side. The food steams in the morning air and my mouth waters in anticipation.

"Thank you, sir."

Alice and I sit down beside the morning fire, and I dig into the food. It burns the hell out of my tongue, but it feels so good on my empty stomach that I can't stop.

"What's your story?" I ask Alice between bites.

"My story?"

"Yeah. How long you been with these guys?" I gesture around the camp with my spoon.

"Not long. A month or so, I'd say." Alice crosses her legs and sighs. "I was workin' at a cathouse down in Alamosa, got myself into a bit of trouble. So I hopped on a train, met a man on the way to Denver, and I've been with him ever since."

"Which man?"

"Tommy." She points across camp at a man still sleeping, his soft snores drifting toward us on the balmy morning air. "He might not look like much, but he's more of a gentleman than most the men I've had the displeasure of meeting."

"And how'd he get wrapped up in all this?"

"Henry." She shakes her head. "Said he was hunting down a bastard outlaw, and Tommy thought it'd be an adventure to join him. So here we are." She stretches her arms overhead and lets out a long sigh. "Enough chat, we'd best get to work. Come on, I'll show ya around."

We're on dish duty this morning. Alice scrubs the breakfast bowls clean in one pail of water, then hands them to me to rinse in another pail. Everyone else is awake now, chowing down and drinking coffee around the fire, and there's no shortage of washing to do.

Henry approaches us when he's done, and the sun on his face turns his eyes light blue. They remind me of Jacob's eyes, making it hard to look away.

"Mornin', Henry," Alice says cheerily.

"Mornin'," he says, handing her his dish. "Miss Allen." He tips his hat to me.

"It's just Daisy," I correct him.

He runs a hand over the pale stubble on his jaw and squints into the morning sun. "We'll be leavin' today, headed toward Coal Creek."

"Is Hopkins there?" The thought makes my heart hammer in my chest.

"Don't know. But we ain't got any leads, so it's the best we can do for now."

"Why Coal Creek?"

"We'll just be stoppin' off there on the way to Canon City. Hopkins was jailed there, so folks are bound to know about him. We hope."

"Why you after Hopkins, anyway?" I ask as Alice shoves another dish into my hands. I quickly dunk it in the pail of water, shake it off, and place it in a bin to dry with the others.

Henry hesitates a moment, then his gaze shifts to Alice. "Can you spare her?"

"Of course. Go on." She slaps me on the shoulder and smiles.

I wipe my hands on my jeans and follow Henry across camp. The morning sun is in our eyes, and we pull our hats low against the rays.

"This all started up in Golden," Henry says. "Steinburn was a deputy there, and he took part in the hangin' of a dangerous outlaw late last year. Fella's name was Hopkins."

I look over at him sharply.

"Was the elder Hopkins brother. The younger brother, *our* Hopkins, weren't too happy about that. So he took his brother's gang for himself, killed a bunch of innocents, and kidnapped Steinburn's wife, Beatrice."

The story sounds familiar, and I recall the newspaper article from the sheriff's office.

"Why didn't he kill her?" I ask.

Henry shrugs. "Hell if I know. Sick bastard like that . . ." He shakes his head.

"And how do you know them? You family or somethin'?"

Henry kicks the dirt with his boot, sending up a puff of dust. "Not quite. I was livin' with 'em at the time. Beatrice was always takin' in strays, pullin' folks off the streets." He smiles, but it don't reach his eyes. "She pulled me outta some hard times." He straightens up and clears his throat. "Steinburn told me to keep an eye on you, make sure you're gettin' along all right." His blue eyes meet mine and I clench my jaw. It'll take some time to get used to those eyes, familiar yet strange at the same time. "I'm sure Ethel will keep you busy, but let me know if you need anything." He smiles and tips his hat. "Daisy."

"Henry."

I remain at the edge of camp and watch him walk away. Reaching into my pocket, I pull out my tin of cigarettes and am disappointed to find it empty. My other pocket, the one I keep my money in, is near empty, and I wish I hadn't spent so many coins at Schilling's saloon. I'll have to find a way to make myself a few dollars, preferably before I become a burden on these folks.

"Daisy!" calls Alice, waving me over from across camp. "We've got a lot to do before we can hit the road," she tells me, and shoves an armful of clothing against my chest. "Wash these, won't ya?" She smiles and pats my arm before walking away, and I wish now more than ever that I had a cigarette.

It takes until the late morning to finish our chores, and as we're walking through camp afterward, I notice what looks like a fiddle case hidden under a quilt in the back of one of the wagons.

"What's that?" I ask.

"What?"

I point out the case.

"Don't know. Ain't no one in camp play the fiddle, least not that I know of." She shrugs. "Best hurry up. We've got more chores yet, or Mrs. Ethel will kick you out before you're even settled."

CHAPTER 8
August 1880

WE'RE ON THE road to Coal Creek before the sun has reached the highest point in the sky. Steinburn and the others returned with more provisions, and we set off as soon as they were back.

The journey takes us all day, but the sky remains clear and we arrive on the outskirts of Coal Creek by dusk.

We immediately go about setting up camp, and I try my best to stay out of the way. These people move around one another like a river around stones. I, on the other hand, disturb them like a rock tossed in a still lake. So I hang back, stay out of the way, and watch as the camp comes to life.

Later that evening, we're sitting around the fire when Tommy pulls out his guitar. His smile is quick and he has eyes that sparkle, and it's easy to get lost in the music when he's strumming on that guitar and singing.

"My papa used to play the guitar," I tell him, and he smiles at me through the flames.

"He ever teach you?"

"Not the guitar. I'm pretty slick on a fiddle, though."

"Is that so?" He stops strumming and hands the guitar to Henry, who's sitting beside him. Henry plucks out a few notes, then starts singing a song that makes everyone around the fire curse and plug their ears. Meanwhile, Tommy stands up and walks away into the dark, drawing curious looks from those of us around the fire, then returns a minute later with that old fiddle case in his hand. "Let's hear it, then."

He hands me the fiddle case, and I get a tingle of excitement in my fingertips as I flip up the buckles and push back the lid. The fiddle inside has been through the wringer. It's nicked and scratched and one of the strings has come loose. I tighten it up as Tommy resumes strumming on his guitar, then rosin the bow and slip the fiddle up under my chin and start to play.

Damn, does it feel good. I didn't realize how much I'd missed this. My fingers dance over the strings, and Alice claps beside me. Burns wanders over from the chuck wagon to listen, and Henry taps his boot in the dirt.

Tommy plays along, matching my tempo and tune. It reminds me of evenings spent around the fire with Papa, playing songs together, watching Mama and Jacob dance. I stand up, puffs of rosin rising off the bow as I saw the strings, and Alice lets out a hoot. She jumps right up, kicks off her boots, and starts dancing around the fire. Henry joins her, and their laughter is contagious. He spins her around so many times that her long black hair comes loose from her bun and tendrils fall around her face. She stumbles, dizzy from the dance, and Henry catches her. When they look in my direction, both their smiles falter.

"What the hell are you doin'?" Ethel asks from behind me. I turn around and she rips the fiddle from my hands so fast that the bow falls in the dirt. Her face is twisted into such an angry grimace that you'd think I kicked her dog or something. "You had no right touching this, ya hear? You'd best keep your hands off what don't belong to you."

"It's just a fiddle," Alice says, hands on her hips.

Ethel narrows her eyes, looks ready to exchange fighting words, but then just lets out a long sigh. "You don't understand," she says softly. She presses her lips into a hard line and looks down at the instrument in her hands. She holds it gently, her fingers wrapped around it with care.

"We're sorry, Mrs. Ethel," Tommy says. "It was my fault. I didn't realize." He takes off his hat and looks at her all gentleman-like.

Ethel gives me one last look, picks up the bow from where it fell in the dirt, and walks away without another word.

"What the hell, Tommy?" I pick up a pebble and chuck it at him. It bounces off his shoulder and he winces. "Why'd you give me that if I ain't supposed to touch it?"

"I didn't know!" Tommy says, lifting a hand to ward off any more stones. "She's never said nothin' about it before."

"You're gonna get me kicked out, and it's only my first day." I sit back down with a huff.

"Oh, you ain't goin' nowhere, darlin'," says a woman behind me. She walks up to the fire carrying a fifth of whiskey and pauses to shake my hand. "Missy Fairfax," she says. She hands me the bottle and then sits down beside me. "Her bark is worse than her bite," Missy says, gesturing in Ethel's direction. The light from the flames dances across her auburn hair and her green eyes, making them shine. "She's just gotta get used to you."

"She still ain't used to me," Alice says. She reaches out a hand for the whiskey and I pass it to her after taking a swig. It burns going down, but it's a familiar sensation, one that's strangely comforting.

"She's got a good heart," Missy says. "It's just hard to find it sometimes."

Ethel doesn't join us for the rest of the evening, nor do Steinburn and Carr. They're locked in a deep conversation at the other end of camp, sitting across from one another at a wobbly card table while their cigarettes burn in the dark. I want to know what they're saying, what they're discussing with such serious faces. Hopkins?

Missy offers me the whiskey bottle, which has been passed around the fire, and I put it to my lips and drink heavily, trying to chase Hopkins's voice from my mind, trying to drown out the gunshots that left my ears ringing and my family bleeding.

The bottle only makes it one more time around the fire before nothing but a drop remains.

"We got anymore?" Alice asks, but Missy shakes her head. "Well, who's it gonna be?"

Everyone spits in the dirt suddenly , except for me. Then all eyes land on me and collective laughter goes around at my expense.

"You're up," Henry says.

"Why me?"

"Last one to spit," Tommy explains, as if it were obvious. Alice is sitting beside him, glowing, and I ain't sure if it's from the whiskey, the firelight, or Tommy's hand on her knee. I wonder if Billy ever made me look that way.

"Go with her, Henry," Missy says. Henry narrows his eyes, looks like he wants to argue, but he doesn't.

He stands up and holds out a hand. "Pay up," he says, and everyone around the fire pulls coins out of their pockets and drops them into his hand. I give him what I can, but there ain't much left after all those nights I spent at Schilling's. That was right stupid of me.

Henry puts the money in his pocket and nods his head to me. "Let's go."

We head to the horses, where Lucky has been eating hay and oats happily since we arrived. He had some arguments with the herd last night and early this morning, but they seem to have settled things. If only folks could work out their problems like horses do. A bit of kicking and squealing, pinned ears and flashing teeth, and then all is settled.

We saddle up and Henry leads the way out of camp. The nighttime air is cool and fresh on my face, and I take off my hat to let it brush through my sweaty hair.

"That's a fine horse," I tell Henry as we ride. He's got a beautiful dappled palomino with a creamy white mane and tail.

"She sure is." He leans forward and pats her on the neck.

"What's her name?"

"Biscuit."

I smirk. "Biscuit?"

"She likes biscuits!" His laughter, combined with my buzz from the whiskey, makes me laugh, too. Papa always said laughter was the best medicine.

"You fancy a bit of a race?" Henry asks once I've stopped laughing, and my heart thrums with excitement.

"I never turn down a race," I say, snugging my hat down over my head. "You ready to lose?"

"Biscuit never loses."

"We'll see about that."

We get the horses lined up shoulder to shoulder, and Lucky trembles with anxious excitement. He paws at the dry dirt and I have to keep tension on the reins to hold him back.

"Ready?" Henry asks.

"Born ready," I say, flashing him a sideways smile.

"Go!" he yells, and both horses bolt forward. Biscuit immediately takes the lead, which I expected. She's bigger than Lucky is, with more muscle in her haunches, but she's heavier, too. I hold Lucky back a bit, letting the palomino take the lead even farther. Henry lets out a cry of victory, as if he's already won.

I smile.

Loosening the reins, I lean low over Lucky's neck and let him really run. He charges forward, determined to catch Biscuit. Lucky is built for this—long legs, hardy hooves, and fire in his heart.

Henry should've known better than to race us.

We blow past him, leaving Biscuit in the dust just as flickering lantern light from the town in the distance materializes out of the darkness.

I slow Lucky down before we get to town, then turn him around so I can see the look on Henry's face as he rides up behind us.

"Shit," he says, shaking his head as he brings his horse to a stop. "Didn't know you could ride like that."

"There's a lotta things you don't know about me," I say. "Guess we should'a bet on that race."

"I'm glad we didn't," he says with a smile.

We continue into Coal Creek, our horses breathing hard, and head down the main thoroughfare in search of the general store. It's a small town, and the people we pass look at us through narrowed, suspicious eyes. Maybe they don't trust the guns strapped to the side of Henry's saddle, or maybe they just don't like the look of us. I tip my hat to a lady and she gives me a scowl so deep it's a miracle her face don't get stuck like that.

Coal Creek, true to its name, is a mining town. The feel of the place is heavy, thick. Most of the men here must work in the coal mines, and their wives probably sit at home during the day just hoping and praying their husbands come home. I remember Mama pacing by the windows while I was growing up, always waiting for Papa to come home. There was only one cave-in during Papa's time at the Merriweather mine, and be it luck or an act of God, he weren't in the mine at the time. But that's the way it is in the mining business— only a matter of time before something goes wrong.

We spot the general store up on a corner, then hitch the horses outside. Our boots are loud on the boardwalk as we climb the stairs and push through the creaky door into the shop.

The owner gives us a nod of acknowledgement, then Henry and I find our way to the liquor shelves in the back.

"How many can you fit in your saddlebags?" he asks. I pull two bottles of whiskey off the wall and hold them up.

He grabs a couple bottles and we go to the front to pay for everything. I nab an apple from a basket nearby and take a bite. Henry glances over at me as I wipe the juice from my chin.

"We'll take the apple, too," he grumbles, but there's a smile playing on his lips.

"Can I see that?" I ask, pointing to a small journal on the wall behind the shopkeeper. He grabs it and hands it over. The cover is tawny brown and the pages are crisp, just waiting to be filled with pictures and words. I trail my fingers across it and let out a small sigh.

"You draw?" Henry asks.

"Used to. Old sketchbook burned up with everythin' else in that fire."

"Make that the whiskey, the apple, *and* the journal," Henry tells the man. He pays him with a handful of coins, and the shopkeeper grumbles as he counts it out.

"You don't gotta—"

"I want to. Maybe you can draw me somethin' some time." He winks one blue eye, making me smile.

"No promises."

We head outside, and there's a man leaning up against the railing on the boardwalk. I step around him, but Henry bumps into him as he passes by.

"You want me to knock your head off your shoulders, boy?" the man asks, lifting a fist. He's got a near-empty bottle of liquor in the other hand, and he uses that arm to wipe the spit from his lips.

"Sorry, sir. No, sir." Henry ducks his head apologetically. "Excuse me." He tips his hat and steps down to the horses. "Let's go," he says. "And don't break those bottles, else I'm not responsible for what they might do to you back in camp."

"I ain't scared'a them," I mumble, taking another bite of my apple.

We're about to mount up when the drunk on the boardwalk yells, "Bastard! You robbed me!" He moves quick for a drunk fella, and he's off that boardwalk and has his hands around Henry's neck before I can blink.

He drags Henry back, away from the horses, their boots stirring up dust. Henry tries to get free, but he's a hell of a lot smaller than the other man, and it's no use.

They scuffle and the man loses his footing, which sends both of them tumbling into the dirt. Henry tries again to get away, but can't break the man's grip. A crowd starts to gather. Some of the men cheer them on, and the others just smoke their cigarettes and look mildly entertained. I take another bite of my apple and lean back against Lucky to enjoy the show.

The men are still going at it, punching each other and twisting around in the dirt. Henry may be younger, but that drunk fella is big and angry, and I don't like the looks of it when he gets Henry pinned and wraps his hands around his throat.

He's gonna kill him, I realize, and I'm the only one who cares to stop it. The man dropped his bottle when they started to wrestle, and I hurry to grab it up, tossing my apple away in the process.

Henry's gasping for breath and the life's going out of him. The men gathered around holler and clap as I flex my fingers around the glass and push through the crowd. With a grunt, I smash the bottle over that bastard's head as hard as I can. He cracks open like a melon, blood dripping down the back of his neck and into the collar of his jacket.

Henry pushes the man's limp body away and sucks in a big gulp of air as I grab his hat off the ground and pull him up by the front of his shirt. He staggers to his feet while the onlookers start to move in, poking and prodding at the man bleeding in the dirt. If he's got any buddies in the crowd, I don't wanna be around to meet them.

"Shit," Henry says, with a bit of a dazed look to his eyes. I put his hat back on his head and walk him to his horse. "Gimme a damn minute," he mumbles, trying to push me away.

"We don't have a damn minute," I whisper as the crowd starts to grow restless. That man in the dirt still hasn't moved. "Get on your horse—*now.*"

I help steady him as he swings into the saddle, then I'm up on Lucky right quick. Henry's still got enough sense to follow me outta town, and I don't stop until we're well into the plains.

"What the hell was that?" I snap, turning Lucky around abruptly.

"That whiskey okay?" Henry asks.

I open my saddlebag to check on it. "It's fine. Now what was that? You robbed that man?"

"I sure did." Henry pulls a billfold out of the pocket of his buckskin jacket. "Five bucks." He's got a broken lip that bleeds across his teeth when he smiles.

"You're a damn fool," I say, but I smile all the same. "Now come on—they'll be wonderin' where we are."

Henry bought me a new journal.

He's a fine man, though I wouldn't tell him so.

D. Allen

CHAPTER 9
August 1880

STEINBURN COMES TO find me bright and early the next morning.

I'm sitting off on my own, slicing up a fresh apple with the knife Mama and Papa gave me, and he takes a seat in the grass beside me.

We're on the bank of a small river, an offshoot of the Arkansas, which we followed west from Rock Creek. The grass grows tall and thick here, and the mosquitos buzz incessantly. I wave them away and pull up the red bandana I wear tied around my neck.

"How you finding things?" Steinburn asks. He props one elbow lazily on his knee and squints into the sunlight shining off the water.

The apple slice I stick in my mouth is sweet and full of juice, and I savor the flavor before wiping my lips and offering Steinburn a slice.

"Everyone's been real nice," I say, and I mean it. "I think I may have ruffled Ethel's feathers a bit, though. Somethin' about that damn fiddle."

Steinburn chuckles and takes the slice I offer him. "Belonged to a fella we called Ol' Jeb. I think she was sweet on him, though she won't say anything about it, even if you ask." He wipes his fingers on his jeans and sighs. "We all have our baggage."

"Some more than others." I clear my throat. "Henry told me about Beatrice."

Steinburn's eyes narrow. He pulls a blade of grass from the bank and twirls it between his fingers.

"I'm sorry," I say, because he clearly ain't gonna say anything. "Sounds like she was a fine lady."

"She still is," he corrects me. "Or I pray she is, anyway." He readjusts his black hat and sits up straighter.

I pick up a flat stone from the bank and skip it across the water, just like Jacob taught me. It makes Steinburn smile.

"I've never been good at that," he says.

"It's all in the wrist," I reply, wiping dirt from my fingertips. Then I tip my hat back and turn to face him. "Henry said we're riding for Canon City. You think Hopkins is there?"

"I don't know where he is, but I wouldn't bet he hangs around Canon City. I just hope he has some buddies there, or some enemies, preferably. Anyone who can tell us where he's headed."

"And if no one knows? Then what?"

Steinburn picks up a stone and tries to skip it, but it hits the water and sinks with a disappointing splash.

We're back on the road, and the trees that surround us as we follow along the Arkansas river stand tall and proud under the summer sun. The oaks that clump together along the trail provide relief from the midday heat, and their dark green leaves shift and rustle in the light breeze.

About a mile outside of Canon City, Steinburn pauses our wagon train to point west, toward where mountain peaks reach for the pale blue sky.

"That's the Royal Gorge," he says, then lets out a long whistle. "A sight to behold, or so I've been told."

"What is it?" I ask.

"One of the deepest canyons in Colorado," Steinburn says. His eyes have a slight twinkle when he tips back his hat and looks over at me. "The first excursion train passed through last summer."

"Beatrice wanted to see it," Missy says softly, almost inaudibly, from where she sits beside Steinburn in the wagon. Steinburn's eyes go dull, and he doesn't say another word until we reach Canon City.

This city sits in a valley bordered on the east by the Arkansas, and shadowed by mountains everywhere else. The Wet Mountains are immediately to the west, with the Sangre de Cristo range just beyond that.

We get to work setting up camp, but I find myself distracted by the giants looming over us. I wonder what it'd be like to climb to the highest peak and look down at the world. From way down here it looks like I'd be able to feel the clouds. Maybe I could even reach up and touch those three bright stars in the sky, the ones I like to pretend are my family looking down on me.

I've just finished hauling water for the horses when Henry, Tommy, and Alice approach me.

"We're gonna head into town," Alice says. "Thought you might like to join us."

"Lookin' for Hopkins?" I ask, feeling a burst of nervous excitement.

"Nah," Henry says from beside me. He's scratching Biscuit's neck and she lets out a sigh of contentment. I like the way he works with her, always gentle, patient. Not many men treat their horses as kindly as he does.

"Why not?"

"Steinburn don't want us asking too many questions. Thinks it'll raise suspicion if Hopkins still has fellas around here."

"So what's the plan?"

"He and Carr plan to hit up a few places, talk to some folks Carr used to know back when he rode with the gang."

"Carr rode with a gang?" My eyes immediately find him, and he's across camp smiling at something Ethel is saying to him. "With Hopkins?"

Henry laughs. "No, course not. Just some bad fellas years ago, back before any of us knew him. A few of them have settled down around here, got into the oil business. Steinburn hopes they might know something of Hopkins's whereabouts."

"So what're we goin' into town for?"

"A *drink*," Alice says, reaching for my hand. I let her take it, and her touch startles me. I ain't been touched since my last time with Billy, and there's something both unsettling and calming about it. Her warmth, her fingers laced through mine—it reminds me of holding Mama's hand back when I was a little girl.

"So, you comin' or not?" Henry asks, narrowing his blue eyes as if it's a challenge. And he may not know it yet, but I never back down from a challenge.

"Yeah, I'm comin'."

We take a wagon into Canon City, and it's bustling even at this hour. It's bigger than Rock Creek, likely on account of the oil struck here. Papa used to buy the newspaper in town, and I remember when he read about all the folks moving to

Canon City, hoping to find a job in oil. Papa and Mama discussed moving the family up the Arkansas, getting into a different business than mining, but we stayed put, and he toiled on as the foreman of Merriweather's mine. Weren't but a couple years back he finally left that business.

He turned to farming instead. Corn and potatoes, mostly. I'll never forget the sound of a summer wind through the corn, softly shushing as if singing a lullaby. If only he'd had more years at it. If only Hopkins hadn't come around.

I know we aren't supposed to go running our mouths off about him around here, but I keep a wary eye out as we roll down the thoroughfare. After parking the wagon, we all climb out and briefly argue about which saloon to visit first. Henry wins the argument, which don't surprise me in the least, and then we're heading through the swinging doors into the saloon.

Men stand in a line along the bar, and sit around tables playing cards. Smoke hangs heavy in the air, casting a yellow haze to the lanterns flickering along the walls. Ladies aren't always welcome in saloons—unless they're working—so Alice and I find a table in a back corner while Tommy and Henry procure us drinks.

"Been saving that five dollars for this?" I ask Henry as he places a glass of whiskey on the table in front of me.

"Sure have. Ain't no shame dippin' into a pocket here and there. Pays for a good time." He smiles as I shake my head.

"So you're a pickpocket. All of you?" I gesture to Alice and Tommy.

"Not me," Tommy says. "I ain't no good at sleight of hand."

"But you're good at other things with your hands. Ain't that right, Alice?"

Alice slaps Henry playfully and rolls her brown eyes. "That ain't none of your business, Mr. McCloud."

We laugh and clink our glasses of whiskey.

"To finding that bastard," Henry says.

"And to killing him," I add.

We drink until Henry only has a few coins left in his pocket. He tosses them to me and then pushes back in his chair, balancing it on the back two legs. "Your turn to buy," he says, nodding toward the bar.

I've had a bit much to drink, but I'm able to find my way through the crowded saloon and then brace myself against the bar.

"One more round!" I call to the barkeep, and he nods. I'm still standing there waiting for the whiskey when a heavy hand falls on my shoulder.

"What do we have here?" says a slurring voice. The man leaning over me is red in the face, his brow gleaming with sweat from the heat in the saloon. "Ain't you a pretty little thing." He smiles and I grimace at his missing front tooth.

I knock his hand off my shoulder and stand a little straighter. The whiskey has my head swimming. Thankfully the bar is helping me keep my balance.

"You'll keep your hands to yourself," I tell him. I touch the knife sheathed at my hip, but it don't seem to bother the man none.

"Ain't gotta be a bitch," the man says. A few of the fellas around him turn to look at us, their eyes narrowed, watchful.

"Here's your whiskey," the barkeep says, sliding a tray of glasses toward me. I give him what's left of Henry's money before turning back to the man.

"You got somethin' on your face," I say.

"Wha—"

I douse him in the whiskey from one of the shot glasses and he stumbles back, crying out as he claws at his eyes. No one bothers to help him, and the other men laugh as he stumbles around, momentarily blind.

When I get back to the table, Henry nods in the man's direction. "What was that about?"

"Must be serious to waste your whiskey on," Tommy notes.

"Just another drunken fool," I say, settling into my chair.

I don't want any more whiskey anyway. What I want is to dunk my head in a barrel of cold water and chase away the fog clouding my mind.

The others continue to talk and laugh, but I struggle to keep up with their conversation. Instead I watch the man from across the saloon, and he watches me. He's here drinking with one other fella, and they both look like they could use a bath—or two. Dirty clothes, unkempt hair, and sallow cheeks hint at a hard life. A life on the road, perhaps.

I watch them until they leave, and then I watch the swinging doors, just to make sure they're gone.

"You okay?" Alice asks, placing her hand lightly on mine. I nod and smile.

"Fine." Sighing, I sit forward and prop my cheek on one fist. "So tell me about this." Alice and Tommy look surprised as I gesture between them. "Met on a train?"

"Oh, yes," Alice says. "We met on the Denver-bound train."

"Where were you comin' from?" I ask Tommy.

"East." He runs a finger along the rim of his shot glass. "Grew up in Pennsylvania."

"Why'd you leave?"

"Wanted more, I suppose." His brown eyes meet mine and he smiles. "Folks always say if you want adventure, you head West."

"And then you met Henry," I say, remembering the story Alice told me when we first met.

"He could probably convince a fish outta water," Tommy says, which makes Henry laugh.

"What about you?" My eyes land on Henry, and his smile fades. "What's your story?"

"Ain't got one."

"We've all got a story," I say. "Don't wanna tell me yours?"

"Some stories aren't meant for tellin'."

He turns away, the outline of his square jaw sharp and unwavering. I shrug, too full of whiskey to care.

"Where you goin'?" Alice asks as I stand up.

"I'll be right back," I tell her. I head out the swinging saloon doors, look up and down the thoroughfare for any sign of those fellas, and then go searching for an outhouse.

I find them about fifty feet from the saloon, far enough away that the smell don't disturb the patrons, but close enough that even a drunk could stumble there if necessary. There're two—one with a crescent moon cutout in the door, and the other with a star. The symbols make it easy to determine which to use, since many folk in the area ain't never learned how to read.

I pull open the door with the crescent moon, hold my breath, and quickly go about my business. Ain't such a luxury as toilet paper around here, but there's a stack of newspapers beside me, and that's good enough. One newspaper says something about the Royal Gorge, but I don't bother to read it before crinkling it up.

After I'm done, I step back outside and walk a few paces before taking a breath. The sky overhead is dark and cloudless, and it twinkles with the light of innumerable stars. As has become my habit, I seek out the three brightest stars in the sky, then reach up as if to touch them.

"Well, well," says a voice from behind me, and I know who it is without turning around. "Guess you came lookin' for me after all."

"Don't flatter yourself, mister," I say as I start to turn around. But before I can, something hard hits me upside the head. The force of it makes me fall to my knees, and for a moment I can't catch my breath. I reach a hand up to touch my head, and it comes away covered in blood.

"You son of a bitch," I mumble, but my vision swims and I can't get my bearings. Shapes and colors are blurring together, melting like butter in Mama's pan. I can't tell which of the men kicks me over and binds my wrists and ankles. I think to scream for help, but a cloth is shoved in my mouth before I get the chance.

"Now, now, little lady. You just settle down, and everythin' is gonna be just fine."

I pull on my binds, but they hold fast. The rope digs into my skin, biting each time I move. I struggle as one of the men picks me up and slings me over his shoulder.

"Oh, stop fightin'," he says. He tosses me over the back of his horse and laughs. "Ain't gonna do you no good."

The swirling colors and shapes go dark, and I drift into a world of black.

CHAPTER 10
August 1880

I AIN'T SURE how long I'm out, but when I open my eyes it's still nighttime and I'm still slung across the back of a horse.

I have Papa's gun with me, tucked into the waistband of my jeans, but I've neglected to buy bullets or learn how to use it. Who the hell carries around a revolver without any damn bullets?

I don't bother trying to scream or cry, as the cloth tied over my mouth prevents anything more than garbled sounds, and besides, there isn't anyone around to hear me scream anyway. We must be a long way from Canon City, because no matter which direction I strain to look, I can't see any lights on the horizon. I wonder if Henry and the others have noticed I'm gone. Maybe they're already on our trail . . . assuming anyone cares to come looking for me.

We descend down a gentle slope into a valley clustered with limber pines. The trees cast long, dark shadows in the moonlight, and pinecones and evergreen needles crunch under the horses' hooves.

We ride into a camp, one that must be difficult to see from the road, and it looks like the fellas have been here for a while. Bottles and cans are scattered about the place, shirts and trousers are hanging on a line between two pines, and the fire pit is charred black and full of spent coals. A wagon covered in a tarp lurks in the shadows, and I wonder briefly what they've got in it.

The toothless man near kicks me in the head as he swings his leg over his horse to dismount, then he yanks me down and tosses me roughly against the base of a tree. He easily finds Papa's revolver and relieves me of it, which makes me seethe with anger and humiliation.

"Look at this," he says to his partner, holding up the old gun. He clicks open the cylinder and laughs. "Not a single bullet." He tosses it to his buddy, who tucks it into the waistband of his trousers. "Not sure what you thought you was gonna do with that," he tells me. He leans in close and takes my chin roughly in his hand. I'd bite him if not for this rag between my teeth. "I'll show you my gun later," he whispers. I wrench my face away and clench my fists behind my back.

He continues to search me, and I pray he don't find the knife sheathed on my side. But my prayers ain't ever answered. The man slides the blade free of the sheath and lets out a low whistle. The knife gleams in the moonlight, and watching the man's grubby fingers wrap around the hilt makes me fight against my binds.

"Fine knife you got here." He clucks his tongue and spits in the dirt. "*D.A.* Those your initials or somethin'?" His eyes turn to me and I glare. How I wish I could wrap my hands around his throat and squeeze until his face turns blue. Then I'd squeeze some more, just for good measure.

When I don't answer, the man kicks dirt in my face. It gets in my eyes and nose, but I can't get a hand free to wipe it away.

The men throw a couple pieces of wood into the fire pit and crack open two cans of beans for supper. My stomach growls as I watch them slop the beans into a cast-iron pot to heat in the flames.

Every so often their eyes drift toward me, and I can see what darkness lurks there.

I've gotta get myself out of here. Ain't no way I'm gonna be a corpse in this place.

The rope around my wrists is rough and tight, and no matter how I pull or shift or turn, my hands won't slide free. If only I still had that damn knife.

They pop open a fresh bottle of something strong, and the knot in my stomach grows. But I might be able to use this to my advantage. Drink slows the mind and the body, and these men are most certainly already slow in the head.

They notice me staring before I quickly look away. The other man, the one with a full mouth of teeth, saunters over, bottle in hand, and kneels down so he can get right up in my face. "We gonna have fun tonight," he says, stroking my cheek with the back of his hand. His breath reeks of whiskey and beans, turning my stomach. I wish I could spit in his damn face, but all I can do is turn my head roughly away. "You look at me when I'm talkin' to you!" he snaps, taking a fistful of my hair and yanking my head around. The pain that shoots through my neck is sudden and fierce and I yelp. This just makes him laugh, like I'm some form of entertainment. He stumbles back toward the campfire, and a single tear slips down my cheek. But I have to keep it together.

I wait for my chance, bide my time. Only when they're good and deep in the bottle do I try to make my escape.

My wrists and ankles are still bound, but I'm able to slowly get my feet under myself. One man walks off into the trees to take a piss, and the other has his back to me. It's now or never.

I stand quietly and begin shuffling away into the dark.

My movements are painfully slow, but if I go too fast I might fall, and getting back up will take longer than I have time for. I shuffle my left foot forward, then my right, barely keeping my balance as I move through the dark. Pale moonlight filters through the trees overhead, guiding my way. The ground is blanketed in evergreen needles, which mask the sounds of my movement.

Step with the left, step with the right. Slowly, slowly.

"Hey, where'd she go?" one of the men asks, his voice drifting toward me through the trees.

Shit.

I strain my eyes in the dark, searching for someplace to hide. There ain't anything out here but trees, so I press myself against one and hold my breath.

Boots crash through the underbrush behind me.

"Where you go?" asks the man in a drunken slur. He's so close—close enough that I can hear his breathing. My hands shake so bad that I have to clench them together to stop the trembling.

God, if Mama's right and you're up there—

"Got you." The man yanks me out from behind the tree and punches me so hard that I lose my balance and hit the ground. My ears ring and my vision swims. The man picks me up by the front of my shirt and hits me again, this time with the back of his hand. The force of the blow sends me sprawling into the dirt. Before I can get up, the bastard grabs me by the ankle and drags me back toward camp. I try to struggle, try to make it harder on him, but it don't do no good. He yanks me again and I mumble a scream around the cloth between my teeth. My hair tangles in the needles and dirt, my clothing rips and rides up as he drags me. But no matter how I fight, I can't break free.

He drags me all the way back to camp and leaves me

beside the fire. "Thought she could run," he says. His toothless partner laughs.

"We ain't even got started. You wanna miss all the fun?"

I pray to just die now.

The man standing over me takes out a knife. It shines in the flickering firelight and I try not to imagine which part of me he'll cut off first. He draws nearer and I strain, trying to pull away, but he uses it instead to cut the binds from my ankles. I try to kick him, but I can barely see straight and miss him entirely.

The world is spinning—just like it did when Jacob spun me too fast on the rope swing in the barn. The man undoes the button on my pants and yanks them off, then tosses them in the fire. Now I'm in the dirt in nothing but my undergarments.

I want to plunge a knife so deep into his throat that he chokes on his own blood. I want to string him up in the tree overhead and watch the light fade from his eyes.

The man climbs on top of me and his breath is foul in my face. I struggle, trying to wiggle out from under him, but he weighs too much, and I still can't see straight. I hit my head hard when I fell, and I can't seem to shake my mind clear.

He yanks the cloth from my mouth and I take in a gulp of smoky air. His lips come crashing down on mine as his free hand goes to his belt. His fingers fumble along the leather, but he's too drunk to get the buckle undone. I use the last of my strength to knee him in the crotch as hard as I can.

"Bitch!" he wheezes, trying to catch his breath. I start to laugh, and he don't like that none. He pulls Papa's revolver from his waistband and positions the grip over my head like a bludgeon.

So this is how it's gonna end—beaten to death by my own damn gun. I should've just shot myself when I had the chance.

I've just barely closed my eyes, waiting for the first blow

to land, when a gunshot splits the air. My face is sprayed with something warm and wet as a bolt of panic shoots down my spine. Every muscle in my body tenses, and all I can think of is that night at home, hiding in the root cellar while shots rang out in the house above me. I think of Mama's body hitting the floor, the sound she made across the floorboards.

Hopkins. His name draws me back into my body. *Hopkins. I have to kill Hopkins.*

Above me, my attacker goes limp. His right eye is shot clean through, leaving nothing but a mangled, bloody mess. I'm covered in his blood—can taste it on my lips. His body falls forward, and his broken face is so close to mine that I can see the fragments of his skull that were shattered by the bullet.

A shadow falls across me and the man is lifted from my chest. Henry and Carr sling the dead man into the fire and then reach down to pull me up.

Henry cuts the rope binding my wrists as Carr removes his calf-length duster jacket and slings it over my shoulders. I pull it tight around myself, its warmth easing my shivers and hiding my state of undress.

"This yours?" Henry asks. He picks up the revolver and offers it to me. As soon as I take it, I realize with a start that I still don't have my knife.

I turn to look around the camp, and the other man, the one who stole it, ain't nowhere to be found.

"Where'd he go?" I ask, turning around and around as if he's hiding somewhere just out of sight.

"Other fella took off," Carr says, his dark eyes narrowed as he stares into the trees. "Soon as he saw us, he was gone."

"He has my knife," I say. I want to be strong, but it comes out as a whimper.

"We can get you a new kni—"

"No," I interrupt Henry. "My mama and papa gave me that knife . . . right before they died." I grip the revolver so hard my hand starts to shake. "I've gotta get it back."

"We will." Carr's voice is unshaken. "But not tonight." I open my mouth to argue, but he holds up a hand. "We'll get your knife back, but we need to get you home first."

That word, *home*, it stops my argument before it's even formed on my tongue.

Henry and Carr search the camp while I watch the man's body burn in the fire. I only wish I'd been the one to put the bullet through him.

"Look at this," Henry calls out to Carr, and I turn my head. They pull the tarp from the wagon to reveal ten whiskey barrels. Henry hops up and pops the top off one, then reels back with a cough. "Moonshine."

Carr joins him, and they open all ten barrels to confirm what we already know—those fellas were making illegal moonshine and selling it someplace, maybe even someplace close.

"What do we do with it?" Henry asks.

Carr is quiet for a long moment. His dark eyes flick up, and he points to the horse tethered to a nearby tree. "Get that mare harnessed up. This'll fetch a high price, and we need the money."

Henry and I exchange a brief glance. Selling moonshine could get us thrown in jail, but running out of money means we can't track Hopkins like we need to.

I harness the mare up to the wagon, noting the marks and scars on her body. She's jumpy, nervous every time my hands come toward her.

"Easy, girl," I whisper while Henry and Carr secure the tarp back over the wagon. "You're safe now."

CHAPTER 11
August 1880

I WAKE UP under a sunset sky. I'm lying in a cot, and it takes me a moment to remember last night, to remember that Henry offered it to me when we got back with the horses and the moonshine.

I start to sit up and pain throbs in my head and behind my eyes. I push my way through it, panting with the effort. Reaching up, my fingers tangle in my blood-soaked hair and I hiss at the pain in my scalp. There's a thin blanket over me, and when I glance under it I realize I still don't have any pants on.

My reflection in the pail of water beside the cot don't look too pretty. Both my eyes are swollen, with dark purple bruises under each. My lower lip is split in the center and has dried blood crusted over it, and there's a deep cut on my cheek that stings like hell.

"Good lord, she's awake."

I look up to find Ethel hurrying across camp toward me. A few others follow behind her: Alice, Tommy, Henry, and even Steinburn.

"Alice, get her something to eat. Hurry now." Ethel sends Alice off in search of food and kneels before me, tucking her long skirt under her knees. "How do you feel?" she asks. She picks up a rag and dips it in the pail of water, then gently wipes the blood from my lips.

"Like shit," I say.

Steinburn is standing behind Ethel with a worried look etching wrinkles into his skin. His dark brown eyes are narrowed. Beside him, Henry and Tommy watch me with similar expressions.

"Here, drink." Ethel hands me a cup of water and I sip at it. The cool water soothes my throat and I don't even mind when it spills down my chin.

"I've gotta get that bastard," I say, my voice cracking painfully. I won't be able to leave this place until I get my knife back.

"We will," Henry says.

"After you rest," Ethel chimes in.

"Where's my gun?" I look around and spot it lying on a crate beside me. Ethel hands it over and I cradle it in my lap. "I didn't have a single bullet," I say, gritting my teeth. "That man would've killed me, and I couldn't even protect myself."

"It's about time you learned how to use that damn thing," Steinburn says. "What good is a gun if you can't even fire it?" I look up at him and his lips twitch into a smirk. "I see how you hold it—like it's an heirloom, not a weapon." He turns to Henry. "Mr. McCloud, you'll teach the girl. And Miss Allen, as soon as you're feeling better, I want you shooting that gun every day, learning how to protect yourself with it. Understood?"

"Yes, sir," I say. He doesn't have to tell me twice. I've been a fool, waiting this long to learn how to use the damn thing. "What about that man? What if someone finds the body?"

Steinburn shakes his head. "Bastards like him don't have anyone to come looking. And even if he did, the animals would get to him before anyone notices he's gone." He spits in the dirt. "We don't like killing if we don't have to, but the situation called for it."

"They deserved it," Henry mutters. "Better off dead."

"McCloud," Steinburn says in a warning voice. Henry just scuffs a boot in the dirt and looks the other way.

"Here, I got you somethin' to eat," Alice says, pushing through everyone gathered around me. Ethel shoos the men away as Alice sits on the cot.

"Eat what you can," Ethel says. "And Alice, help her with that water."

"Yes, ma'am."

Ethel leaves me alone with Alice. She helps me eat and drink, but my jaw hurts so bad it's hard to chew.

"Henry told me what happened," Alice says softly. "Those men, did they . . . you know . . ."

"No," I say sternly. "Bastard couldn't get his own damn drawers off."

Alice lets out a relieved sigh. "They sure did a number on you, though." She reaches for the cloth to dab more blood away from my face. Once she's helped me with one more sip of water, she fluffs my pillow and leaves me to rest. "Just holler if you need me," she says before walking away.

I lie there staring at the canvas lean-to over my head, running my fingers across the gun resting on my chest.

I'm gonna learn how to shoot the damn thing, and then I'm gonna kill that toothless bastard and pry my knife from his cold, dead hands.

The day slipped away as I slept, and now an endless expanse of stars twinkles overhead. The air has a chill to it that hints of the coming fall. I curl my toes and shiver under the thin blanket.

There's cigarette smoke in the air, and it makes me want

one. With a groan, I sit up in the cot and squint into the dark. Henry sits nearby, leaning against a wagon wheel while he stares off into the dark.

"You're up," he says when he notices me.

"So are you."

"Can't sleep."

"You can have the cot back. I've overstayed my welcome as it is." I make to get up, but Henry waves me off.

"It's not that," he says. "Most nights are like this. Ain't got no one to blame but me." He stands and pulls a cigarette from the tin in his pocket. "Want one?"

"Badly."

He lights it up and sits on the end of the cot before handing it to me. I pull my legs out of the way, wrapping the blanket around myself to ward off the cold.

We sit there together in silence for a while, watching the gray smoke drift into the night sky.

"Thanks for . . . everything," I say.

"Ain't no need to thank me for that." He looks over and gives me a small smile.

"How'd you find me, anyway?"

"We tracked you as far as we could, but the campfire smoke gave it away. Those two morons sure weren't keen on coverin' their trail."

"Which of you shot that man?" I ask, remembering the perfect hole right through the man's eye.

"Carr."

I take a puff and let the smoke out slow. "He's an impressive shot."

"That man could shoot the wing off a butterfly."

"And what'd he do with the moonshine?"

"Took it a couple towns east—Farley went with him. Should be back in a day or two."

I nod as we lapse back into silence. It's comfortable sitting with Henry, reminds me a bit of sitting on the porch with Jacob back home.

"Why can't you sleep?"

"Bad dreams." He flicks ash from the end of his burning cigarette. "You probably know all about that."

I nod. "Had one about Mama the other night." Tears spring to my eyes and I wipe them roughly away. "Not sure which is worse: wakin' up knowin' they're dead, or thinkin' this has all been a bad dream."

"I dream about my mama, too."

"She dead?"

"Nah. My pa is, though."

"Sorry."

"Don't be. He was a cruel bastard." Henry finishes his cigarette and grinds it into the dirt with the toe of his boot. "Get some sleep," he says, giving me a hint of a smile. His blue eyes are bothered—the smile doesn't quite reach them.

He stands, and the cot is colder without him beside me. I watch him walk into the dark, hands in his pockets, and wonder what story he's got to tell.

CHAPTER 12
August 1880

THREE DAYS LATER, my face still looks like a bruised plum, but I'm back to my duties around camp. I would've been back to them sooner, but Ethel insisted I take it easy.

When I've finished feeding and brushing all the horses, I go in search of Henry. We ain't talked much the past few days, not since I asked about his mama. I find him sitting on his cot, a letter open in his hand.

"Mornin'," I say, and he squints up at me.

"Mornin'." He folds up the letter and tucks it into his pocket. "Need somethin'?"

"I want you to take me shootin'. You free?"

"No. Can't ya see how busy I am?" He gestures at his cot, which I miss like hell now that I'm sleeping on the ground again. "I was about to take a nap."

"Naps are for children and old men." I kick his dusty boot. "Get up. Let's go."

"You're a pain in my ass," he grumbles, but he stands up and puts on his hat anyway. I shove his shoulder playfully and get a smile in return.

We gather up the empty beer bottles scattered around the fire from last night and put them in a crate, then walk a short distance down to the river. This section of the Arkansas is wide and slow moving, and thick trees grow along the banks. A cool breeze lifts my hair from my neck and I sigh into its gentle touch.

Henry sets the crate down and the bottles clink together. The sound reminds me of a windchime Mama used to have hanging on the front porch. It used to make such beautiful sounds in the evening breeze.

"Here, set these up on that stump over there," he says, handing me a few bottles. I line them up carefully and return to him.

"You ever shot before?" he asks.

"No."

"Not once?" He looks surprised. "Damn. Seeing the way you ride, I'd expected you to shoot a gun better than the rest of us, too."

"All in time."

He laughs, and the sound is warm and gentle. If he weren't making fun of me, I might actually like it. "Well, what'cha waitin' for? Let's see that gun."

I slip Papa's gun from the waistband of the long skirt I'm wearing. I ain't got no money to buy myself new jeans, but Alice was nice enough to lend me something of hers.

I hand Henry the gun and he fishes a handful of bullets from his pocket. "All right, now listen. To load a revolver, first you open this latch here." He flips open a door that reveals a spot to put a bullet. "You load one bullet into each chamber. There's six of 'em. Then you rotate the cylinder and load the next one." He slides a bullet into the chamber and turns the cylinder to reveal the next empty chamber.

After loading all six, he shuts the door again and everything clicks into place. "Now it's loaded. You got that?"

"Easy enough," I say with a shrug.

"Pull the hammer down, and you're ready to fire. You squeeze the trigger and it's gonna go off, so make sure not to be aimin' at your feet or nothin' while you're loading it."

"Ain't that obvious?"

"You'd be surprised. Here. Be careful, now." He hands me the gun, and it feels heavier than before. I don't know if the bullets weigh it down, or if it's just my perception. "Hold it steady," he says. "Use those sights up top to aim at your target."

I lift the gun, its weight unsteady in my hands.

"Hold it like this." Henry carefully readjusts my hands so that my pointer finger is stretched out long and straight across the side of the barrel. "Don't put your finger on the trigger until you're ready. Then breathe out slow, and squeeze."

I get a bottle in the distance aligned between the two metal sights. I cock the hammer, pull the trigger, and *bang!* The gunshot rings in my ears and my wrists snap back with the force of firing.

"Damn," I say, shaking out my hand. "Does that happen to you?"

"Nah, I don't have scrawny wrists like you." There's a hint of a smile in his voice. "Besides, I've been shootin' for more years than you've been alive."

"You have not," I say, aiming the gun to try again. "How old are you, anyway?"

"Twenty-one."

I pull the trigger and miss by a mile. I'm not sure where the bullet goes, but it sure as hell don't hit any of the bottles.

"I'm nineteen," I say. "Who taught you how to shoot?" I steady my hands, aim, and fire. I miss again. "Dammit," I grumble. That bullet went left and lodged itself into the trunk of a tree.

"You was sayin' before?" Henry starts to chuckle.

"Shut up."

"No one taught me," he says, answering my question. "I needed to learn, so I learned."

Now I'm even more determined. This time, I'm gonna hit that bottle. I lift the gun, level a bottle in my sights, and pull the trigger. My bullet goes left and hits the tree again. I empty all six chambers, and I don't hit a single bottle. By the time I'm done, Henry's howling so hard with laughter that he's doubled over with tears streaming from his eyes.

My body's on fire with frustration and humiliation. I thought for sure I'd be a straight shot, but I didn't hit a single goddamn bottle.

"Let me try again," I say, holding out a hand for more bullets.

"Ain't no way in hell," Henry replies, wiping the tears from his eyes. "Let you waste my bullets like that? Over my dead body."

"That can be arranged," I say.

"You couldn't shoot me if you tried."

"Asshole," I mutter, and march back to camp without him.

Canon City, Colorado
August 1880

D. Allen

CHAPTER 13
August 1880

HENRY TOLD EVERYONE in camp what happened, and now none of them will shut up about it. I spend the rest of the day fuming, and the rest of the night, too. I'm the new favorite joke around the campfire.

I don't get it. I did everything like Henry told me to—aimed down the sights, breathed out slow, and pulled the trigger at the bottom of my breath—yet I couldn't hit a single bottle.

I'm still upset the next day, and I'm scrubbing a pan like it wronged me when Steinburn comes calling.

"Good morning, Miss Allen," he says. He looks impeccable with his groomed beard and fresh jacket. His eyes are bright and sparkling, which I find questionable at best.

"Mornin'."

"I'm headed into town," he says. "Thought you might wanna ride along, pick up some bullets while we're there." He winks a dark brown eye at me.

"Sounds right nice," I say, "but I ain't got no money." I avert my eyes, shame burning in my belly. Mama and Papa never liked asking for loans, or borrowing of any kind, and I hate this helpless feeling that's come over me. The money I got from selling Sassy is long gone, spent thoughtlessly on whiskey and cigarettes.

"Carr and Farley were able to sell off that moonshine for a nice sum," Steinburn says as he reaches into his pocket. "Wouldn't have found it if not for you." He counts out a stack of bills and hands them to me. "Seems only right you get your share."

I take the crinkled bills as Steinburn claps me on the shoulder.

"Now come on. Let's go buy some damn bullets."

A short while later we're riding down the dirt road into Canon City, the sun high and bright overhead.

It feels strange to be in town again—I haven't been back since those two fellas nabbed me. But the city looks different during the day. People walk the boardwalks, dogs nap in the shade, and children chase each other down the thoroughfare with voices ringing out above the clamor.

We find a place to hitch the horses, but my skirt gets tangled on the saddle horn as I dismount. I must flash half the damn city before I finally get it untangled.

"Goddamn skirts," I grumble.

Steinburn laughs. "Go buy yourself some clothes, then

meet me at the gunsmith when you're done. I'll show you what bullets you need."

The general store is nearby, and I wait for a wagon to pass before hurrying across the road and down the boardwalk. The air is thick with heat and dust, and I push my hair off my sweaty forehead before stepping into the shop. The man inside greets me with a pleasant smile.

"What can I do for you, miss?"

"Need clothes," I say, glancing through the shop. There's a jar of peppermint candies on display, and I help myself to a handful, which makes the man quirk a brow.

"Those are for the children," the man says as I pop one into my mouth. "Ladies clothes are this way."

"No more skirts. You got denims?"

His lips press into a thin line. "Of course, miss."

It's not long later that I've bought new clothes—a loose shirt, fresh socks, and comfortable jeans.

I thank the shopkeeper and head outside, then cross the road and shove the old clothes in my saddlebag. Steinburn is sitting outside the gunsmith halfway through a cigarette when I arrive.

"Those look nice on you," he says, gesturing to my new clothes. "Seem to suit you better, don't they?"

I hook my thumbs through the belt loops and smile. "Sure do."

He finishes his cigarette and holds the door for me as we step into the gunsmith.

The walls sparkle with shiny new firearms. There're so many different types, I wouldn't know where to begin. Pistols, revolvers, shotguns, rifles—enough firepower for a small army.

There's one in particular that catches my eye, a revolver made of darkened steel and accented with a creamy pearl handle.

"Let me try that one," I tell the gunsmith. He looks at Steinburn as if I need his permission, which makes hot anger flare in my belly.

"Go on," Steinburn says. "Give the girl what she wants."

The man takes the revolver off the wall and hands it to me. I flex my fingers around the grip, and it fits my hand like a silk glove. Not that I've ever had one—they're useless, frilly things. But this gun? I could use it to end Hopkins's life, and there ain't nothing more useful than that.

"How much is it?" I ask.

"Seventeen," the gunsmith says, then spits into a spittoon at his feet. Even with the money Steinburn gave me, I still don't have enough. Begrudgingly, I put the gun back on the counter. Watching him wipe it down and put it on the wall makes my fingers clench. It feels like everything I want is just out of my reach.

"We'll take a few boxes of your forty-fives," Steinburn says. "And a holster." He glances over at me with a clever smile. "Every gunslinger needs one."

"Gunslinger?" I shake my head. "Haven't you heard?"

"I heard," he says, "but we've all gotta learn."

I pay for the goods and we step back out into the summer heat. Steinburn hands me the holster and the boxes of bullets, and when I open one up, I'm mesmerized by the sunlight gleaming off the bullet casings. I run a finger over the new bullets and wonder how many will go to waste before I actually hit something.

Steinburn claps me on the shoulder. "You'll be a gunslinger in no time. Now, I got some other business to attend to. You need me to ride back with you?"

He's probably asking because of what happened with those men, but I square my shoulders and shake my head. "No, I'll be fine."

"All right, then. I'll see you back at camp."

"Wait," I say as he turns to leave. "This business—it got anythin' to do with Hopkins?"

He pauses, lets out a little laugh. "Sure can't pull a fast one on you, Miss Allen."

"I wanna go with you," I demand, but Steinburn shakes his head.

"No."

"Why the hell not?"

"Carr and I got business with some men he used to run with—no good men, dangerous men." He gives me a soft smile. "If they know anything about Hopkins, we'll find out, but I can't bring an army of people in there with me, else they aren't gonna tell us a damn thing."

I let out a sigh, my shoulders falling. "I wanna help," I say softly. "All this waitin' and wonderin' is gonna drive me mad."

"Then focus on that gun. Practice until you can load it in your sleep. And keep yourself busy, Miss Allen. Worrying yourself silly won't help any." I stiffen when he squeezes my shoulder. He leaves me standing on the boardwalk, a holster in one hand and my bullets in the other.

I fetch Lucky and am on my way out of town when I spot a man at the livery struggling with a rambunctious red mare. He can't seem to get her into the barn, no matter what he does. It becomes a tug-of-war, and the old man is on the losing end. The mare yanks her head and sends the man sprawling in the dirt.

"Ah, to hell with ya!" he snaps at her. "You ain't worth the trouble!"

The mare's eyes are wide, frightened. That's what prompts me to hitch Lucky to a post and head over.

The man dropped her lead rope when he fell, and I pick it up while he lifts himself out of the dirt.

"Easy, girl," I whisper to the mare. She eyes me warily. "You like candy?" I pull a peppermint from my pocket and unwrap the shiny foil before offering it to her on a flat palm. The mare sniffs it, her ears turning forward curiously. "That's a good girl. Go on, take it." Her soft lips brush my palm as she takes the candy. I give her one more, then prompt her to follow me for a third. She's still cautious, wary of the barn, but she trails behind me. The livery owner opens up a stall for me to put her in.

"Well ain't you a horse whisperer," he says as I close the stall door.

"It don't take a genius to see she was scared." I toss her lead rope at him and he fumbles to catch it.

"Name's Willy," he says, holding out a hand.

"Daisy." We shake.

"Say, I could sure use some help around here, if you're interested." He glances over at the mare and I note the nervousness in his eyes.

"What kind of help?"

"The payin' kind." He smiles. "This mare ain't gonna bring me a dime if no one can get close to her. If you train her up for me, I'll pay ya well."

I cross my arms and study him. He's a round fella, well-fed, probably makes good money selling and boarding horses. My slice of the moonshine money is already running low after today, and I sure could use a steady flow of cash to buy more bullets.

"How much?"

"Fifty cents a day. And I'll need help with the mucking."

Of course he will. "Fifty cents a day for mucking and training?"

"Yes ma'am." He spits in his hand and holds it out to me. I do the same and we shake. "Then I'll start today."

Willy pays me fifty cents for my day's work, and I tuck the coins into a pocket of my jeans. My hands, which haven't held a shovel in weeks, are blistered and red from all the mucking I did today, but it felt good. It's nice to feel needed, even if all I'm needed for is horse shit.

Lucky stands quietly while I tighten up the cinch, and as I do I catch sight of someone over the top of the saddle.

My stomach drops and my fingers falter. The man hasn't seen me—hasn't even looked in my direction. He's riding by, eyes squinted into the evening sun, and has my knife still sheathed at his side. The sight of it hits me like a punch to the gut.

Heart racing, I shift to peek under Lucky's neck. The man is headed farther into town.

Leaving Lucky where he's hitched, I set off to follow the man at a safe distance. He dismounts and hitches his horse outside the same saloon we were in a few nights ago. I'd be daft to go in there after him, so instead I sit on a bench outside the general store to watch. Time creeps by, and I get so antsy waiting that I abandon my post to buy cigarettes in the store. They help, though, and I'm near done with my second smoke when the man steps out of the saloon.

I reach for the revolver at my side and slip it from the holster. All six chambers are loaded, and all I'd have to do is take aim and pull the trigger. Then I'd have my knife back, and he'd never hurt anyone again.

But my hand shakes as I cock the hammer, and I know I couldn't hit him from this distance. I can't even hit a bottle on a stump, let alone a moving target in low light.

With a frustrated sigh, I carefully release the hammer and slip the revolver back into my holster. Not tonight . . . not yet.

Whores whistle and flaunt themselves on the balcony of the cathouse across the way, and the man heads in that direction. The thought of any woman having to undress that vile man makes my stomach turn. But he'll be occupied for a short while, at least, which gives me an idea.

Tossing away my cigarette, I head across the road and push through the swinging doors into the saloon. The place is already full, with music from the piano playing off-key and smoke hanging heavy in the air. Ladies in short skirts serve drinks to men around poker tables and pretend not to care when a rough hand reaches for something it shouldn't.

I ask for a beer and give the bearded man beside me a dirty look when he mumbles something under his breath about it not being a woman's place. The drink I'm given is tall and dark, and it goes down like water on a warm summer day.

I've gulped half the glass before I stop to catch my breath. The bearded man nods like he's impressed.

"Barkeep," I call, raising a hand to draw the man over.

"Another?" he asks. I pull a quarter from my pocket, which is more than double the price of my beer, and hold it up in the lantern light.

"I wanna know about one of your patrons. Man missin' his front teeth, just stumbled outta here a few minutes ago."

The barkeep narrows his eyes and glances at the quarter. "Information ain't cheap."

The bearded man beside me chuckles as I narrow my eyes. Fine, I'll play his game.

"Fifty cents, and I'll take one more beer while you're at it." I clink two quarters down on the bar and the barkeep smiles. He pours me another drink and leans in close. Lowering his voice, he says, "Man's name is Seth. Piece of shit, if you ask me."

"If you ask anyone," the bearded man says. The barkeep ignores him.

"Comes through town every few months. Ain't ever here long, and spends money like you wouldn't believe." He lets out a whistle and jostles the quarters in his palm.

Ain't here long? I squeeze my fingers into a fist. I'd best get my knife back before he hits the road.

"Usually comes in with another fella," the barkeep continues, "but I ain't seen him around in a few days."

That other fella is crow food by now, and better off for it.

"Where's he stay?" I ask. "He got a place around here?"

"Hell if I know." The barkeep shrugs and takes the rag from his shoulder.

"Then what good are you?" I ask, slamming my clenched fist down on the bar. "Gimme my quarters back, ya crook."

"I could have you escorted out, miss, if you'd prefer not to finish that drink?" He eyes my second glass and I grit my teeth and scowl. "Pleasure doin' business with ya." He saunters away, jiggling the quarters as he goes.

"Thievin' bastard," I grumble.

The man next to me shifts on his barstool and glances over while I sip my second beer. I turn toward him and prop an elbow on the bar. "What?"

He finishes his whiskey and runs a hand over his mustache and down his beard. "You gonna kill him?"

"What's it to you?"

"If you're gonna kill him, I might know a thing or two."

I study him through narrowed eyes. "I ain't got any more quarters, so if you've got somethin' to say, say it."

This makes the man laugh. "You're a hell of a thing, ain't you?" When I don't reply, he goes on. "Seth does business with suits from outta town."

"Suits?"

"Rich folk. Got them shiny pocket watches, you know, the kind with the chain." He demonstrates and I roll my eyes. "Rough fellas, not the kind I'd like to cross. I seen him meetin' up with 'em."

"Where?"

"Behind the hotel," he says, jabbing a thumb over his shoulder.

I trace the rim of my glass with a fingertip. "Why're you tellin' me this?"

The man looks over his shoulder before turning back to me. "I seen him with all that moonshine, and he seen me lookin'. Now it's just a matter of time." He draws his thumb across his throat.

"You think he'd kill you?"

The man laughs, short and rough. "I *know* he would. Seth is a foul fucking bastard."

I reach up and touch the split in my head, remember being bound and tossed over the back of a horse.

"I ain't afraid of him," I growl, my stomach burning with rage at the memory of that night.

"Then do us all a favor." The man lifts his glass as if to toast me with it. "And fill him full of lead."

CHAPTER 14
September 1880

I PRACTICE SHOOTING every moment I'm free. Bullet casings litter the riverbank beside the Arkansas, and that poor tree to the left of my stump is torn to bits, its bark ripped off and bullets lodged in its trunk. No matter how many rounds I put through this damn gun, I can't seem to hit where I'm aiming.

Working for Willy has become a necessity. Every day after work I take my fifty cents and head across the road to the gunsmith to buy another box of bullets. Hell, I'll probably buy up the entire stock of forty-fives before the month is out. Assuming we're still here in a month.

Carr and Steinburn ain't had any luck getting leads on Hopkins. All they've found out is he was released from the penitentiary in October of last year, and he left town without telling a soul where he was headed. We're out of ideas, out of leads, and very nearly out of money.

I learned recently that Steinburn's been funding this whole damn thing, and his pockets have run dry. Alice has since gone back to work at the whorehouse, despite Tommy's blatant and fervent disapproval, and the others are still floundering, trying to find work before we go belly-up.

These thoughts and worries keep me awake at night, and I've been lying here fretting about them as the sun comes up over the horizon. Pushing to my feet, I grab the old towel Ethel gave me and stumble down to the river to bathe. Sunrise colors dance on the slow-moving water as I peel off my clothes and drop them in a heap on the bank. The cold water brings some life back into me as it creeps past my shins, my thighs, my belly button. The sandy river bottom is soft between my toes, and I dig my feet into it to keep from being carried away by the gentle current. Goose bumps rise on my arms as a cool morning breeze lifts off the water. Birds are singing in the trees, and if there was ever a place where I could forget about my sorrows, it'd probably be here.

I splash water on my arms and face, washing away dirt and grime from the past few days, then take a breath before dunking myself fully. The cold steals the air from my lungs and I break the surface with a gasp.

Water drips on my feet as I pat myself dry on the riverbank, and something down the way catches my eye.

It's Henry, peeling out of his shirt, reaching for the buckle on his jeans. His body is lean, his muscles defined—it's the type of body only a rugged life can beget. Though I'd like to let my gaze linger, I force my eyes away. I wonder if he saw me bathing, saw my naked skin under the light of the rising sun. The thought brings warmth to my cheeks. It's been too long since a man last touched me.

I think of Billy often, of his lips on mine and his weight between my legs. Late at night I miss him most, when everyone in camp is asleep and I'm lying there alone and cold and scared. But it's better this way. It has to be.

When I get back to camp, Burns is getting breakfast ready at the chuck wagon, and Missy is sipping coffee next to a softly burning fire. Coffee is exactly what I need right now.

"Mornin'," Missy says, her voice rough and husky. "Want a drink?"

"Don't mind if I do." I sit down beside her at the fire and she pours me black coffee. It's hot going down my throat, and although it's bitter, I savor the flavor. There's nothing quite like sipping coffee beside a fire in the early hours of the morning.

Missy doesn't say much. We drink our coffee quietly while the rest of the camp stirs to life. Steinburn shaves his face in preparation for the day, Carr sits under a tree polishing his gun, and Tommy snores softly from his cot on the edge of camp.

My eyes pause on Ethel, and I watch as she finishes taking stock of the supplies in our wagons. She does this every morning, and always walks away with a troubled frown. This morning her shoulders sag under the weight she bears.

"Ethel!" I call out, and she startles. I hold up my coffee cup and beckon her over.

"What is it, Daisy?" she asks. Her voice is tired, worn.

"Ain't nothin' a good cup of coffee can't make better." I grab her a clean mug and pour it to the rim. "Go on. Sit."

Her eyebrows draw down over her eyes, wrinkles forming in the corners, but she finally gives in. She sits with a sigh and I hand her the mug.

"Thank you." She takes a sniff of the coffee and a smile pulls at the corners of her weathered mouth.

The three of us sip from our mugs while watching the sun come up over the river. Henry appears over the hill not long later, his shirt buttoned only halfway, and he catches my eye. Instead of looking away, I smile. His lips curve up and he tips his hat to me before walking by.

Beside me, Missy lets out a short, quiet chuckle.

"So," she says, her green eyes turning toward Ethel. "What do we need?"

Ethel takes one last sip of her coffee before answering. "Beans and grain for the horses, provisions for Burns, medical supplies, and a whole lot of other things we can't afford." She runs a hand over her hair and lets out a troubled sigh.

"Is there anything I can do to help?" I ask quietly. "I'm makin' fifty cents a day. I could buy some things."

"That'd be mighty kind of you," Ethel says. "Every little bit helps." She pats me on the knee like Mama used to, then stands and pours herself another cup of coffee. "But if you really wanna help, bring me a big bag of gold." She winks one eye playfully before she goes. I watch her walk away, noticing the holes along the bottom of her skirt where it barely touches the ground. Missy nudges me when she's gone.

"You okay?"

Her question startles me. Missy ain't ever tried to start conversation with me before. "I'm fine."

"Sure you are." She pushes a strand of auburn hair off her forehead and breathes in the morning air. "Beatrice was my sister, you know. So you and I, we have some things in common."

"Was?"

Her green eyes narrow and her nails clink against the coffee mug as she fiddles with it. "They all think she's still alive." Missy smiles sadly. "William, he'd go to the end of the world for her. But I can't see it—a man like Hopkins carting a woman around with him, especially one so outspoken and stubborn as Beatrice." She laughs and wipes a single tear off her cheek. "No. I think she's been dead a long time."

"Have you told Steinburn that?"

"Sure, but he don't like to hear it. So I keep my mouth closed. Better to let him hope."

Hope. It's the one thing that keeps us going in all this. Hope . . . and rage.

"I hope you're wrong," I say.

"I hope I am too."

I'm down to the grits, so I pour out what's left in my cup and then stand and stretch. My back aches from sleeping on the ground, and I've got a full day of shoveling ahead of me. But before I head to town, I need to get some practice in.

"I'll see ya around," I tell Missy, and she lifts a hand in farewell. I think I like her more now than I did before.

I've got a pocketful of bullets and Papa's revolver in the holster at my hip. I swear to God if I don't hit one of those bottles today, I might just have to shoot myself. At least Ethel would have one fewer mouth to feed.

The gun shines in the sunlight, and I take my time to load the bullets one by one. When all six chambers are filled, I take a deep breath and try to calm myself.

The green bottle, the one I've been trying to hit for days, winks in the light dancing off the river. I try to picture my bullet flying straight and true, shattering the bottle into glittering pieces.

After another deep breath, I line myself up, carefully take aim, and shoot.

"Goddammit," I mumble when the bullet goes far left and rips yet more bark from that poor cottonwood. I cock the hammer and try again. This time when I fire, the bullet goes high and lands off in the river with a frustrating splash.

The river rocks behind me crunch and I whirl around.

"Easy," Carr says, holding up his hands. "It's just me."

"Sorry." I let out a frustrated breath and lower the gun. The green bottle winks its beady little eyes at me. I aim again, trying to ignore Carr watching me, and fire. A bullet casing clatters to the ground as the bullet sinks into the trunk of the tree. "Always left," I grumble. "Maybe I ain't got my head on straight."

"Let me see that," Carr says. He holds out a hand and I give him the revolver.

"Ain't no use," I say. "I'm hopeless."

Carr lines up his shot, aims, and misses.

My mouth nearly hits the ground. I saw him shoot a man clear through the eye socket, and yet the green bottle evades him.

He don't seem bothered by it. He tries again, and misses again. His bullets hit the same spot in the cottonwood tree. With squinted eyes and a narrow mouth, he looks down the sights and shakes his head.

"Your sights are off," he says. "Probably why your pa stopped usin' it."

"What?"

"Here." He pulls out his revolver and hands it over to me. "That's too big for ya, I know, but try it out."

"Don't laugh," I say. I line myself up in the same spot where I stand every day, pull the hammer, let out a slow breath, and fire.

The bullet hits the bottle and shatters it into hundreds of little pieces. Glass litters the ground and shines in the sunlight, and my heart pounds a bit faster.

"Holy shit . . ." I mutter.

Behind me, Carr laughs.

The discovery that it's been the gun all along makes my head spin. I tried a few more times with Carr's revolver, and I hit every damn bottle he set up for me. He told me he'd take my gun in today and have the sights straightened out, and I nearly kissed him full on the mouth.

I'm late getting to the stables, but Willy hasn't even

arrived yet. The horses greet me with hungry whickers, and I find myself whistling as I toss hay into their stalls. This work reminds me of home—horses snorting as they eat their morning hay, dust swirling in the shafts of sunlight streaming through the open barn doors. I used to get up early every morning to make special mashes for Lucky and Sassy, and then I'd find a place to sit and sketch in my book until Mama called me in for breakfast. What I wouldn't give for some of her flaky biscuits right about now.

Lost in thought, I'm sweeping hay out of the barn when a thunder of hooves sends the pebbles around my boots dancing. Stepping out into the sun, I hold up a hand to shield my eyes. A stagecoach has just rolled into town, flanked on both sides by no fewer than six riders. The riders are covered in dirt from a long journey, and the horses sparkle with a sheen of sweat. There are two men up on the bench seat in the coach, one to drive the horses and another acting as shotgun. They've got sharp eyes, dirt etched into their skin, and pistols on their sides.

I lean the broom against the barn door as the men climb down. The driver takes off his gloves and holds out a hand.

"Mr. Matson," he says. "And this here's Mr. Wilkes."

Wilkes nods in greeting, then slings his shotgun up on his shoulder. That wagon must have something damn valuable inside to have a shotgun rider *and* a convoy.

"Call me Daisy," I say, giving Matson's hand a firm shake. "How can I help you, sir?"

"Need a place to keep the horses, and the coach, if possible."

"All of 'em?"

"Yes ma'am."

I let out a low whistle. This'll make Willy a rich man.

Behind him, the door on the coach swings open and two young women step out. They wear finely tailored dresses and have spotless, pointy-toed boots. One woman has blond hair and blue eyes, and just looking at her reminds me of how much I don't have. From the hat on her head to the soles of her shoes, she's near dripping in wealth.

"What a fine day," she says, holding up a gloved hand to shield her eyes from the September sun. Even her hand motions are languid, as if she spent her young life practicing how to twist and flick her wrists in an acceptably feminine way. "It's a good day for a walk. Mr. Matson, you'll handle the horses?"

"Yes, miss."

She gives him a smile and her eyes meet mine briefly. They sparkle in the sunlight, but not as brilliantly as the silver chain around her neck. I can't stop myself from wondering how much money it's worth.

"The hotel is this way," the other woman says. Her dark skin has a shine of perspiration, and she dabs it away with a folded linen square. "We should get out of this sun."

"Let's enjoy it," the blonde replies. She turns up her pale face and smiles as the light washes over her. "Winter will be here before we know it, and we'll wish we'd enjoyed the heat while it lasted." Her companion's lips pinch together, but she doesn't disagree.

The two women turn and drift away. Wilkes follows a few steps behind, his shotgun still resting over a shoulder, and half the riders accompany them at a distance. The remaining riders dismount and linger, looking to Matson for direction.

"Well?" Matson asks, calling my attention back. "You got room?"

"Of course," I say. "Let's get these horses cleaned up."

We get the horses put away in a spacious corral, and Matson counts out enough money to board them for the week. He's not sure how long they'll stay, but assures me he's good for the money and will return to pay for another week if necessary. He pays a bit extra to store the stagecoach, and tips his hat to me before he leaves. He and the rest of the men head into town, their boots kicking up dust as they go.

I jingle the handful of coins in my palm, wondering what

it would feel like to take one. Just one—that'd be enough to buy an extra loaf of bread to take home tonight. Besides, Willy ain't here, so he'd have no idea how much Matson gave me. It'd be easy.

The coins shine in the sunlight streaming through the open barn doors, and I glance around quickly before slipping one into my pocket. It don't weigh nothing, yet that single coin is heavier than I ever expected it would be.

Mama would take the paddle to me if she saw. But I remind myself that this is all for them, my family. These folks I'm with are my best chance at finding Hopkins, and I can't let a little bit of money keep me from that goal. If I need to steal a single coin here or there to make sure we have food in our bellies, I'll do it.

Willy shuffles into the barn soon after, and I give him what's left of the money.

"Well done," he says, giving me a pat on the back. "But those corrals still need shoveling." He winks and sends me on my way with a shovel, and I can't help the bolt of excitement that goes up my spine when he counts out the money and pockets it without another word.

I'm working the skittish mare in the round pen when Matson shows back up. His hair is freshly combed and his mustache has been trimmed, and the clothes he's wearing are finer than the dirty things he showed up in. He's still got that pistol on his side, but his entourage and the two young ladies ain't anywhere around.

"Whoa," I say gently to the mare, taking a step back. She turns in from the rail and flicks her ears forward. "Good girl." I pull a peppermint from my pocket and hold it out to her.

"Fine lookin' horse," Matson says as he slings his arms over the top rail of the round pen.

"She sure is." I pat her on the neck before turning toward him. "Can I do somethin' for ya?"

"No. Just forgot something in the coach is all." He gives me a brief smile before heading around to the other side of the barn, where we've got the coach parked in the back. I stay where I'm at, tipping my head back to look at the peach-colored sky as the sun sinks toward the horizon.

It'll be autumn soon—nights are getting colder, and the sun disappears earlier every day.

Autumn weren't ever my favorite time of year, because it meant summer was over and winter was on its way. Oh, how I hate the bitter cold. But I'd give anything to spend one more winter night with my family, bundled up around the fire into the late hours of the evening. We used to take turns waking up to put on more logs, and I always bellyached when it was my turn. How spoiled and ungrateful I was. If only I knew how limited my time would be with them. I would've done so much differently.

I'm about to send the mare off in the other direction when Matson comes back around the barn.

"Find what you was lookin' for?" I ask.

"Sure did." He tips his hat to me before walking back up the thoroughfare into town.

With the sun slipping lower in the sky, I cluck my tongue and send the mare off on another lap around the pen.

I swing by the general store after work and am able to buy two loaves of bread thanks to the extra coin. I'm thinking about how happy everyone'll be when I step out onto the boardwalk and hear screaming. Down the way, a man bursts out of the cathouse pursued by five angry whores. He trips on the way out, landing flat in the dirt, and the whores are on him like crows on a corpse. I, along with all the other folks who've paused to see what the ruckus is about, watch as the women beat the man senseless. By the time they're done, he's a moaning, bloody mess.

"You ever come back here again, we'll kill you," one of the whores threatens. They all spit on him and then turn and march back inside, the door slamming resolutely behind them.

A woman who stopped beside me to watch sighs as she turns away.

"What was that all about?" I ask her.

She pauses, glancing back over her shoulder at the man. "He may have refused to pay. But more than likely he hurt one of them girls. That's the only time I've known them to beat a john in the streets." The woman clucks her tongue before continuing on her way.

My stomach twists—that's the cathouse where Alice works. Loaves of bread tucked under my arm, I hurry down the boardwalk and try the knob, but it's locked.

"Hey!" I yell, pounding a fist on the door. "Everything all right in there?"

The door swings open and a stern-faced woman glares at me. "We're closed," she snaps. She makes to slam the door, but I wedge my boot in the doorjamb.

"My friend Alice just started here. I wanna make sure she's okay."

The woman's sharp expression shifts. She glances over her shoulder and then opens the door just wide enough for me to slip through. "Come in."

It takes a moment for my eyes to adjust to the low lighting. The cathouse smells like perfume, whiskey, and sex, and low voices float down from a room on the second floor. I don't wait for the woman to show me up.

"Alice!" I take the stairs two at a time and push through the girls gathered around one of the bedrooms. My heart twists when I step inside.

Alice sits on the edge of a bed, naked except for a sheer

robe draped across her shoulders, and she's holding a blood-stained rag to her nose. When she looks up and sees me, tears pool and slip down her cheeks.

"Daisy, I—" She flinches and chokes on the pain.

"What happened?" I ask, barely concealing the rage beating in my chest.

"It was that man," says one of the girls beside me. "He's always been rough, but ain't never done nothin' like this before."

"You know he's rough, yet you let him back in here?" I snap as the madam pushes through the assembled girls.

"We're in the business of making money," she says, her smug nose so high in the air that she'd drown if it were to rain.

"Then maybe *you* should've taken him to bed," I growl. The whores look at me like I've grown a second head.

Alice barely has time to get dressed before the madam throws us out the front door.

"You don't come back here until your face is healed," she says, looking at Alice. "And you." She narrows her sharp eyes and then spits on my boots. I lunge for her, but the door slams before I can get my hands around her too-thin neck.

"Bitch!" I yell at the closed door. Behind me, Alice whimpers.

"I'm sorry," she says, wiping tears from her brown eyes.

"What for?" I readjust the loaves of bread, surprised I didn't smush them.

"Now I ain't got no money." Her lower lip quivers, and she's about to burst into tears.

"Don't you worry 'bout that." I pull her in for a hug, and she holds me tight. "We'll figure somethin' out."

Now I wish I'd stolen more than a single coin.

We ride home on Lucky together, Alice's arms wrapped around my waist. She doesn't say much, and I don't ask her to.

When we get back to camp, I help Alice down before retrieving the loaves of bread from the saddlebags. As I turn back around, Alice's arms crush me in a hug.

"Thank you," she says.

"I didn't do much."

"You did more than anyone else ever has." She pulls away and wipes the moisture from her cheeks. Her nose is swollen and bruises are forming around her eyes, but she still finds it in herself to smile.

"Alice?" We turn, and Tommy's eyes go wide. "What happened?" He holds his arms out and she steps into them.

"I hate that place," she whispers to him as I start to walk away. "I don't ever wanna go back."

Her words, though not meant for me, twist something in my gut. It makes my blood boil to think of Alice, naked and trembling, as he took his rage out on her. If only the whores had killed him where he lay.

I find Ethel helping Burns at the chuck wagon, and she glances up when I drop the two loaves of bread on the table before her.

"What's this?"

"Made a little extra today," I lie. She don't need to know I stole the coin that helped me pay for these. "Thought it'd be a nice break from Cookie's slop."

"My slop is keepin' you alive," Burns grumbles as he walks around the wagon carrying a cast-iron pot.

"You should know better than to insult the cook," Ethel says. Her lips turn up in a smile as she peels the paper away from the first loaf of bread and takes a whiff of it. Her stomach grumbles in response. "Oh my," she says with a small laugh.

"Hopefully two is enough. I'll try to get more of what I can this week, especially since Alice won't be makin' anything now."

"What?" Ethel's smile vanishes. "Why?"

"Some john beat her bloody today. The madam kicked us both out and told her not to come back until—"

Ethel drops the bread on the table and immediately goes in search of Alice. Burns and I watch her go, like a mother bear off to protect her cub.

"Here." Burns pushes a bowl of cabbage soup into my hands. "Try not to choke on it." His voice is gruff, but his lips quirk up in the corners.

"Thanks, Cookie." I take my bowl and one loaf of bread over to the fire.

Farley is waist-deep in a story when I sit down, but no one seems particularly interested in what he has to say. Henry's more invested in picking dirt out from under his fingernails with the tip of his knife.

"What's he goin' on about?" I whisper.

"Who the hell knows?" He glances up and his eyes land on the loaf. "Is that bread?"

"Sure is. Take a piece and pass it around."

Henry rips off a chunk and then tosses it to Steinburn while I start into my supper. It's not near as good as Mama's cabbage soup, but it hits the spot.

"You bought this?" Steinburn asks as he pulls a bit of bread from the loaf.

"Sure did. There's another one over at the chuck wagon."

Steinburn's smile is sad, and I ain't sure why. "Thank you, Daisy."

I nod, then use a finger to wipe the last few drops of soup from my bowl. "You seen Mr. Carr?" I ask, casting a quick glance around camp.

"Sure," Henry says. "Heard he was headin' into town to get those sights fixed." He glances up at me and the firelight casts a playful glow across his eyes. "Maybe you're not as shit as I thought."

"We'll put an apple on your head and find out." I slap him hard on the shoulder and he lets out a hiss, nearly slicing his thumb off with the knife. "Careful now," I say. "Don't want yourself gettin' hurt."

He flips me the bird, but there's a hint of a smile tugging on his lips.

I drop my bowl off at the chuck wagon and then go in search of Carr. I find him sitting in his tent, slowly writing a letter by lantern light.

"Evenin'," I say, hesitating outside.

He finishes what he's writing, then looks up at me. He's got dark scruff along his jaw and wrinkles around his brown eyes. He must be about Papa's age, maybe a bit older. I wonder if he fought in the war, too.

"Got those sights fixed," he says. He waits for the ink on the page to dry, then carefully tucks it away with his books and journals. I didn't realize he was such a learned fella. Even I ain't never had so many books as that.

Carr steps out of the tent, then pulls Papa's revolver from his holster.

"Got 'em all straightened out. You shouldn't have no more trouble."

I bring the gun up and look down the sights, and it's clear now that they were off.

"Thank you. What'd it cost?"

Carr pulls a tin of cigarettes from his pocket and lights one up. "I traded for it."

Of course he did—none of us have enough money to go around paying gunsmiths for craftsmanship like this.

I slip the gun into the empty holster at my waist and hold out a hand. Carr looks at it curiously as the tip of his cigarette smolders.

"I'll pay you back," I say as he puts his hand in mine. "One way or another."

CHAPTER 15
September 1880

BACK AT THE livery, I work myself to the bone under the summer sun, cursing the heat on my skin and the sweat that drips from my brow. After cleaning the corrals, I sit down for a break in the shade next to the barn. It must be half past noon when I spot them rich folk coming out of the hotel down the thoroughfare.

The women carry dainty parasols with pastel ribbons that flap in the breeze. They wear different dresses from yesterday, and the idea of owning a separate dress for each day of the week makes me smirk. Mama would've loved to see me in one of those. They look elegant, but so cumbersome, too. The women lift their skirts in one hand and hold their parasols in the other, and I feel tired just watching them as they cross the road and step into the general store.

Matson and Wilkes stand outside smoking cigarettes while they wait for the ladies. They glance once in my direction, though I doubt they can see my eyes from here, so I keep on staring.

I've never much liked rich folk, and a tickle of irritation creeps up my neck as I watch them. Maybe it's because I know now, more than ever, what it feels like to be dirt poor. If it weren't for the kindness of Steinburn and the others, I'd probably still be sleeping on the roof of the barn back home. Or, more than likely, I would've shot myself already.

I continue to watch them as the ladies finally exit the store and head in my direction. The men linger at the back while the blonde steps forward to greet me.

"Good afternoon," she says, her pink lips turning up in the corners.

"Afternoon," I say, tipping my hat.

"We've come to see the horses," she says.

Before I can reply, a young boy comes running down the thoroughfare, kicking up dust as he goes.

"Ms. Merriweather!" he shouts, and the name shoots a bolt of surprise down my spine. "Miss, you forgot your candy." The boy holds out a bag of candies wrapped in silver foil, and the woman smiles as she reaches for them.

"Thank you kindly. What would I do without you?" She bends to plant a kiss on his dusty cheek and the young boy goes bright red.

Merriweather. I can still hear the name on Hopkins's tongue.

Then the gunshots, the blood, the fire. The end of my life as I knew it.

The boy turns and dashes back toward the general store. With some difficulty, I rearrange my face into a neutral expression, hoping no one saw the shock that I'm sure was clear as day. The women step up to the corral fence and Matson whistles for the horses. The woman unfolds the silver foil with delicate fingers, then holds out the peppermint candies on a flat palm for the horses to take.

Merriweather. The name runs through my mind on repeat,

and I can't forget the convoy of riders she arrived with. Could she be one of them?

Lucky puts his head over the adjacent fence and nickers for a candy, pawing impatiently at the dirt.

"What a beautiful pinto," the woman says, reaching out a hand to let Lucky sniff her.

"Thank you."

"Oh, he's yours?"

"Yes, miss. His name's Lucky."

"May he have a treat?"

I nod and she fishes another candy out of the bag and hands it to him. He crunches loudly and nickers for more, making the lady laugh.

"They all seem very happy," the blonde says after having looked over the horses.

"I'd hope so. I do my best to keep them comfortable."

"Thank you for that, Miss . . . ?"

"Daisy."

"Pleasure to meet you, Daisy. My name's Elizabeth." She holds out a dainty hand, and I hesitate a moment before shaking it. I'd have thought she'd be averse to touching something so dirty as I am. "This here is my friend Lily," Elizabeth says, gesturing to the woman behind her.

"You're mighty quiet," I say.

"I prefer listening over speaking," Lily says. "You learn more about people that way." She looks at me like she's looking right through me.

"How are you enjoyin' Canon City so far?" I ask, turning away from Lily. "Not too boring for you, I hope."

"Not at all," Elizabeth says. "It's certainly quaint, but it has a certain Western charm that I find quite appealing."

"You stayin' long?"

"No, unfortunately not." She sighs and pats Lucky's nose. "We're on our way back home. Come from Chicago to see Daddy, and now we're headed back. We've just come from down south, near Pueblo."

"Your daddy must be in the mining business," I say, and Elizabeth's blue eyes narrow slightly.

"What makes you say that?" Her voice is sweet, soft, but Lily shifts uncomfortably behind her.

"My papa used to work in the mines down in Pueblo. Was foreman for a while. Maybe you've heard of it—the Merriweather Mining Company?"

"Well, what a small world this is," Elizabeth says, and some of the tension seems to drop from her shoulders. "Seems our daddies worked together."

"Sure did."

"If your family is down south, why are you up here?"

"My family don't live there anymore. They were murdered, 'bout a month back. Man named Hopkins."

Elizabeth doesn't so much as blink an eye, but Lily's head snaps toward me so quick it's a miracle she don't break something.

So they know his name. What else do they know?

Elizabeth reaches out and takes me by the hand. "I'm so sorry to hear that. I can't imagine what you've been through."

"Hell," I say, pulling my hand away gently.

"What did you say your name was again?"

Either she wasn't listening the first time, or what she's really after is my family name.

"Daisy. Just Daisy."

I watch for a reaction, but Elizabeth only smiles. "Well, Daisy, I appreciate all you've done for us here. And I'm so sorry to hear about your family. You'll be in my prayers tonight."

I force my lips into a smile. "Much appreciated, miss."

Elizabeth turns and opens her parasol with a snap. Her two waiting escorts brush the dust from their coats.

"We'll meet again soon, I'm sure."

I tip my hat to her, aware of Lily's eyes on me before she turns to follow Elizabeth.

Elizabeth Merriweather.

That woman knows something about Hopkins—I can feel it, just like I can feel a storm the day before it hits.

And if she knows something, I'm sure as hell gonna find out what it is.

CHAPTER 16
September 1880

I 'M FINISHING UP with the mare in the round pen as the sun sinks toward the horizon. I've not been able to get Elizabeth's face, or name, out of my mind.

When I said Hopkins's name, she acted as though she'd never heard it before. But Lily—Lily let the cat out of the bag. I keep going over our conversation in my head, trying to pick apart everything Elizabeth said, every movement she made and smile she faked. I have to find out what she knows about Hopkins. Steinburn ain't had any luck, and this might be our last chance to pick back up on Hopkins's trail before it's too late.

I've just put the mare up in her stall for the night when I step out of the barn and spot Seth riding by, a packhorse in tow. Stepping back, I hide against the open barn doors until he's past.

Bastard, I think, my fingers going to the empty sheath I still wear on my side.

And then everything clicks together, and I wonder how I've not seen it before now.

Seth is meeting with the Merriweathers—tonight. The man at the saloon told me he'd be meeting with some rich folk, but I never made the connection. I ain't never been so grateful for loose lips.

I leave Lucky at the livery and continue into town on foot. The sun will be down soon, and if Seth's meeting up with Elizabeth, I'm gonna be there.

My heartbeat quickens and my mind is running faster than a Thoroughbred. What does Seth have to do with Elizabeth, with the Merriweathers? What does Elizabeth know about Hopkins? Does she know why he murdered my family? I've got too many questions and not enough answers.

He glances in my direction and I spin around and pull my hat low, pressing my back against a wooden beam on the boardwalk. A couple is walking by and I give them a brief smile before peeking over my shoulder.

Seth finishes checking the saddlebags on the packhorse and then pushes through the doors into the saloon. I hang back, pace the boardwalk outside the general store. My hands shake, and I smoke a cigarette to calm my nerves as the sun sets. When I've smoked it to a stub, I grind it under the toe of my boot and step into the thoroughfare.

The lamplighter hasn't come through yet, so I'm able to slip up beside the packhorse concealed by shadow. I run my hands over her neck and shush her, then glance quickly toward the saloon before unbuckling one of the saddlebags and looking inside.

My breath hitches.

The saddlebag is full of cash.

Seth must have horse shit for brains. Who'd leave this much cash hanging around in a saddlebag?

The saloon doors crash open behind me, startling the horses so they pull on their leads. Two men throw a third out and he lands hard on his back.

"And stay out," one of the men growls, "or else next time I'll toss your body to the pigs."

Seth pushes himself up from the boardwalk, a bit wobbly on his feet, and I quickly duck behind the packhorse. There's a line of horses hitched outside the saloon, and I use them as cover, shuffling away in the dark before Seth can spot me.

Crouching between two bays, I listen for Seth as he picks up his hat and steps into the dirt.

"Bastards," he mutters. "All of 'em." He spits in the dirt and I hold my breath, fear paralyzing me to the spot. I recall his hands on me, binding my wrists, throwing me over the back of his horse. I can still feel the weight of that other man as he pinned me to the ground, his lips crushing mine.

My revolver pulls smoothly from its holster and I hold it in my right hand, thumb hovering over the hammer. I won't ever let that happen again. I'll blow a bastard's lights out before he can get his hands on me.

But Seth don't even see me. He checks the saddlebags, swings onto his horse, and rides off down the thoroughfare. He's headed toward the hotel, just like the old man mentioned, and I need to get there before he does.

Ducking into the shadows, I slip between the saloon and the gunsmith and run through the ankle-deep grass behind the buildings. It swishes around my boots as I glance around corners, making sure I'm staying just ahead of Seth.

The hotel is at the end of the thoroughfare, a two-story building with double doors and flowers blooming in hanging planters along the deck. It's lined with windows, and candlelight flickers in the rooms beyond.

I've gotta stay low and out of sight. If Elizabeth or any of her men see me, this will all be for naught.

I pause behind a building and peek around the corner. Seth is still coming down the thoroughfare, moving at a slug's pace. There are a couple of outhouses off to my left, and I hurriedly slip behind them, making my way slowly toward the hotel.

I kneel in the grass, holding my breath to keep the rank smells from killing me. One more peek around the outhouse confirms Seth is still far enough away that I should be able to sneak by unseen.

My thumb resting on the hammer of my revolver, I steel my nerves and make a break for it. I don't look over my shoulder, don't glance up to see if I've been spotted out a window. I don't stop running until I'm pressed against the back wall of the hotel, my heart racing and my breathing ragged. I hold my breath, listen for Seth pursuing me, or the Merriweather escorts coming through the grass to see what I'm sneaking around for.

Crickets chirp softly in the dark and a coyote sings from somewhere far-off.

With a sigh of relief, I glance around for a better place to hide. The grass back here grows tall, untouched by horses and wagon wheels. I sink down to my belly and crawl on my elbows and knees to a dark spot tucked into a corner. From here I'm able to glance around the back where, if the old man was right, Seth should be meeting with the Merriweathers.

I prop my revolver up in the dirt, careful not to let the metal flash in the moonlight. My heart continues to race.

Then I wait.

Seth comes gimping into the clearing behind the hotel soon after, lugging the saddlebags from the packhorse. He drops the bags in the deep grass and rolls out his shoulders.

It don't take long for the others to arrive. Elizabeth moves through the grass as though she don't even touch the earth, like her feet are floating beneath the pale blue gown she wears. Her blond hair hangs in waves down her back, and she wears elbow-length white satin gloves.

Matson and Wilkes walk beside her, and a few nameless

men spread out around the clearing. I lie motionless in the tall grass, fighting the urge to swat a mosquito from the side of my neck.

"Miss," Seth says, removing his hat. He fidgets with it, shifting his feet uncomfortably as Elizabeth reaches out a hand for the book Matson carries under his arm.

Wilkes hauls over a barrel from nearby and sets it down before Elizabeth. She uses it as a makeshift table, placing the book on it and leafing through the pages with a bored expression.

Seth clears his throat. "It's, um, a mighty fine honor to meet you, miss. May I call you Elizabeth?"

"No," Matson says.

Seth looks between Elizabeth and her escorts. "Where's, uh, where's Bill? I usually meet with him."

"He's dead," Elizabeth says, not glancing up from the book. She finds the page she's looking for and runs a gloved hand across the paper.

"Dead?"

"That's what I said." She looks up, her pale hair shining like a halo in the moonlight. "Someone killed him. Thought you might know something about it."

"Me?" Seth laughs, but no one else does. "I don't know nothin' about that."

"Pity." Her lips pinch. "No matter. You know what you owe us."

"Yes, miss." Seth grabs the saddlebags and hands them to Matson, who kneels in the grass and starts the tedious task of counting out the stacks of money. Elizabeth doesn't budge. Her eyes remain on Seth, and he squirms under her stare.

It feels like an hour passes by the time Matson finally stands and whispers something in Elizabeth's ear. She removes her gloves and writes something in the book, and I itch to get my hands on it. Maybe there's something about Hopkins hidden in those crisp pages.

Elizabeth looks up and Seth chews his lip. "Where's the rest of it?"

Crickets chirp in the silence that follows.

"Well, miss, we nearly had it, you see." Seth looks down, scuffs his boots through the grass. This ain't the same man who struck me with a bottle and threw me over his horse. This here's a quivering boy.

"Then where'd it go?" Elizabeth asks. She stands with impeccable posture, her shoulders thrown back and her spine ramrod straight.

"The shine—it was stolen before we could sell. And they killed Ralphie, too. Would've killed me if I hadn't—"

"You lost it?" Her voice is barely more than a whisper.

"No, miss, it was stolen, like I said."

"By whom?"

"I don't know. Ain't never seen them before. They was just comin' through town, and—"

Elizabeth slams the book closed, making me and everyone else in the clearing jump. Thankfully no one's looking in this direction. All eyes are on Elizabeth as she grips the sides of the barrel. She gives Matson an almost imperceptible nod, and he steps forward and punches Seth across the face.

Seth stumbles and falls, a hand held to his bleeding nose.

"What the hell wa—"

"Who was it?" she asks, her soft voice at odds with her white-knuckled grip.

"I don't know!" Seth says again, his voice wavering as blood trickles across his lips. "Shot Ralphie clean through the skull. I ain't seen them before in my life. Please, miss, it weren't my fault. You've got to belie—"

"Matson, Wilkes." The men stand to attention as Elizabeth slips her gloves back on. When they don't move, she tilts her head, catlike. "Well?"

I hold my breath as the men grab Seth. He tries to scream, but they shove a rag down his throat, just like he did to me.

They drag him into the shadows and take turns beating him while the rest of Elizabeth's men look on. This would be hard to watch, *should* be hard to watch, but he's getting what he deserves.

Elizabeth doesn't bat an eye. She watches, her expression neutral and unreadable, as the men kick and strike Seth's writhing body. They don't stop until he's gone still.

Matson pulls a handkerchief from his pocket and uses it to wipe the blood from his hands while Wilkes straightens his jacket.

Elizabeth hands the book to Matson. "Another shipment, lost." She slams a fist down on the barrel. "First Pueblo, now here. He's one step ahead of us."

"We'll find him," Wilkes says.

"And when we do," Matson adds, "we'll kill him."

Elizabeth turns with a sigh, her skirt whispering over the grass. "You'd better," she says. "Or else I'll find someone who can."

Matson grabs the bags of cash and the men follow her back to the hotel, leaving me in the grass, my revolver still poised and ready.

I don't so much as sigh until they're long gone. Slowly, quietly, I push up to my knees. Seth still ain't moved from the shadows.

My revolver out, braced in my hands, I creep toward the trees. His body is lying there, his hat abandoned where it fell.

"Mister," I whisper, glancing over my shoulder to make sure no one's watching from the hotel. The windows are empty, the curtains closed. "Hey, mister."

I prod him with the toe of my boot, but he don't move. The hilt of my knife peeks out from under the hem of his torn, bloody shirt, and the sight of it makes my breath catch.

Keeping my revolver on him, I kneel and reach forward. My fingers wrap around the hilt of the knife, the feel of it familiar against my skin, and I pull it free.

Seth's hand snakes out and snags my wrist, but this time

I'm ready. I cock the hammer with a satisfying *click* and level the barrel of my revolver at his forehead. When his shifty eyes look down the muzzle, he slowly releases my wrist.

"You," he says after spitting out the bloody rag they shoved in his mouth. He starts to cough, and dark droplets splatter the grass. I take a step back, knife in hand. "You did this."

"No," I say, "but I wish I had."

"You're the reason Ralphie's dead. You're the reason I'm—" Seth coughs again, his words stolen away. His breathing sounds wet, like there's blood in his lungs. He ain't got long left.

"Who are they?" I ask. "And what's in that damn book?"

Seth doesn't even look at me. He lays his head down and continues to wheeze. I prod him with my boot again, but he don't react.

"Hey, don't go dyin' on me yet. What do you know about the Merriweathers? About Hopkins?"

Seth lets out one final breath, and his body sags, his chest falling still.

"Bastard," I growl. "Good for nothin'." I kick him, hard, right in the gut. Blood trickles from his parted lips, but he don't move.

Knife in one hand and gun in the other, I turn and look back toward the hotel.

I'm gonna get that ledger, and when I do, it's gonna lead me right to Hopkins.

CHAPTER 17
September 1880

WHEN I GET back to camp, I find everyone around the campfire.

"We can't keep goin' on like this," Farley is saying. He picks up his bowl and tosses it on the ground, spilling beans into the dirt. "I can't live on beans and rice, Steinburn."

Steinburn sits on a log, staring into the flames. The others sit around him, their faces drawn.

Henry stands. "We can't give up," he says. "Beatrice would never leave us behind."

"What makes you think she's even alive?" Missy asks softly. Steinburn's eyes cut toward her, hard and sharp. "I mean it," she says. "We might be chasin' a ghost."

I bite my lip as I swing out of the saddle. If it were Jacob who'd been taken, I'd have chased Hopkins and killed him out of spite. What's it matter if Beatrice is alive or dead? Shouldn't Missy want him to pay for what he's done?

"We don't know that," Henry says. His hands are fisted at his sides. "What if she is alive? We can't leave her . . ."

"I agree," Ethel says. "Beatrice would never abandon us. It wouldn't feel right, givin' up on her now."

I pull off Lucky's saddle while I listen to the exchange. My heart races, my blood pounds through my ears. If they give up on Hopkins, what'll I do? How will I go on alone?

"We're out of money," Steinburn says. His voice is weary, his eyebrows drawn down. "And we don't know where he is. All our leads have run dry, and none of our contacts know a damn thing about his whereabouts."

"I know someone who might."

All eyes turn toward me as I step up to the fire.

"Who?" Steinburn asks.

"You got any of those beans left?" I ask Burns, and he gives me a brief smile before going to fill a bowl. "It's a long story," I say as I take a seat beside Alice, who's wrapped in a blanket. "Starts with them moonshiners."

"We've gotta get that book!" Henry says, waving his hands wildly.

Steinburn paces the length of the fire with his arms crossed. "We don't even know if it's Hopkins she was talking about," he says. "Any number of gangs could be tormenting them and stealing their products."

"It *has* to be Hopkins," I cut in. "Before he shot my papa," I continue, trying to control the fluctuations in my voice as I remember that night, "he mentioned Merriweather."

"It makes sense," Henry says. "Hopkins is getting his revenge, just like he did on you."

Steinburn's jaw clenches, his eyes swirling with a mix of anger and pain.

"We can't walk away," I say softly. "Not when we're so close."

"Close?" Farley lets out a rough laugh. "We ain't even laid

eyes on the fucker since he left Steinburn bleedin' with a bullet in 'im.''

Steinburn's hand immediately goes to rub at a spot on his left shoulder.

"He shot you?" I ask.

In response, Steinburn unbuttons the top of his shirt and pulls the fabric away to reveal a twisted scar, about the size of a bottlecap, in the front of his right shoulder.

"It's a miracle that bullet didn't kill him," Ethel says softly.

"He took your wife and tried to kill you, and you'd give up?" My hands shake, my knee bounces. It takes everything I have not to explode, not to yell and cry and ask how he could be so stupid, so *weak*.

"We don't have any more money," Steinburn says, calmly buttoning his shirt.

"The Merriweathers have more money than we'd ever be able to spend," I tell him. "That bastard gave 'em two saddlebags of cash. All we'd need is one."

Steinburn lets out a rough laugh. "Now you want to take their money, too?" He shakes his head. "We'd be damn fools to get involved with the Merriweathers. We'd be exchanging one enemy for another—an enemy more powerful than Hopkins will ever be."

"I'd rather *die* than let Hopkins get away with what he's done. Let the Merriweathers come—I ain't afraid of them."

"You don't know what you're saying," Steinburn says. "You don't have any idea what a man like Merriweather is capable of."

"I don't care," I say. "If Hopkins hit their stash in Pueblo, then he's likely to hit another. We have to get that book and find out where their next drop-off is. It's our only chance."

"Why didn't Hopkins come here, then?" Tommy asks, his voice small and curious. "We took the moonshine, not Hopkins."

We all lapse into silence as the question settles over us. I hadn't thought of that. What if he just hit the one stash? What if he doesn't plan on hitting another? What if—

"He'd never come back here," Carr says. He's been so quiet, lingering in the shadows, that I forgot he was even here.

"Why not?" Henry asks.

Carr's cigarette smolders in the dark as he flicks ash into the dirt. "He was jailed here for eight years. Even a man like Hopkins wouldn't be keen to return after that."

"You would know," Farley says, letting out a rough laugh, but Carr don't respond. Instead he stands, grinds his cigarette under his boot, and levels his gaze on Steinburn.

"I'm with Daisy."

Carr and Steinburn stare at each other. It's as if some secret, silent language is passing between them, and none of us understand it.

"You'd risk everything?" Steinburn asks. "Would bring Merriweather down on us?"

"For Beatrice?" Carr nods. "I would."

Another beat of silence passes as the fire crackles and pops.

"Then it's decided." Steinburn turns toward me. "I hope to God you're right."

CHAPTER 18
September 1880

WE SQUAT AROUND a map hastily scratched into the dirt with a stick. A lopsided square depicts the hotel, surrounded by other tiny squares that are supposed to be the rest of Canon City.

I listen intently as Steinburn and Carr toss out ideas and come up with our plan. This'll take six of us to pull off, and even then I ain't sure it's gonna work. But what choice do we have? If Elizabeth has what she came here for, it's unlikely she'll stick around for long. We need to get our hands on that book, and we ain't got time to waste.

"Does everyone understand?" Steinburn asks, looking at each of us in turn. Tommy chews his nails, Henry twirls a throwing knife between his fingers, and I just hope this ain't the night we all die. I've got to kill Hopkins before that can happen.

"Then let's saddle up."

Silence falls over us as cinches tighten up and dusty boots step into creaking stirrups. My hands shake, and I squeeze my fingers into a fist and will my nerves to settle. I have to stay levelheaded—we all do.

Alice reaches up to Tommy, takes his hand in hers, and places a kiss on it. He leans down to kiss her and my stomach pinches.

He'll come back, I think, but I don't say it aloud.

"All right, folks." Steinburn adjusts his hat and turns his horse around to face us. He sits tall in the saddle, his broad shoulders pulled back as he regards each of us in turn. "You each know what you have to do. We work together, we get that damn book, and we get out. Ain't no one gonna get hurt. Soon we'll be on the road, and all of this will be behind us."

Henry takes off his hat and howls like a wolf to the moon, which lessens the tension a bit.

"Let's ride!"

We gallop out of camp, the worried eyes of the women following us as we go. I focus on the feel of Lucky beneath me, the roughness of the leather reins in my hands, the way the pale moonlight turns us all slightly silver as we ride toward town. I keep imagining jail and hangings, dusty boots dangling six inches off the ground. But I can't get distracted. I have to stay focused, for all of us.

No one speaks as we near Canon City. The moon is high but the night is young. The brothels and saloons will be busy at this time of evening, and prying eyes are always lurking in the shadows.

We slow our horses to a walk and head for the livery, the first building on the south end of town. A lantern hanging outside the barn doors flickers with firelight, lighting my way as I swing out of the saddle and push the doors open.

"Who's there?" comes Willy's rough voice. I find him leaned back in a chair, his boots propped on a crate, a Twain book in one hand and a glass of whiskey in the other. "Oh, Daisy. Don't you know better than to creep up on a man?"

"You read?" I ask as he takes a sip of whiskey.

"Course I read. How else am I supposed to get a bit of

adventure 'round here?" He waves the book, gesturing at the sleepy livery, with the horses breathing evenly and the mice crawling through the rafters overhead.

Boots whisper in the dust behind me and Willy's eyes go wide.

"Sorry about all this," I say.

We tie Willy up, put a bandana in his mouth, and toss him into an empty stall. He lands in a pile of hay, then squirms around to look up at me. His eyes burn and he fights the fabric between his teeth.

"I'm sorry," I say again as I close the stall door and lean over it to look at him. "It was either this or kill ya." The anger in his eyes is briefly replaced with surprise, and I smile and tip my hat before stepping away.

"Where's the coach?" Farley asks.

"Back here."

I lead the group around the back, where the Merriweathers' coach waits in the dark.

"Grab a lantern," Carr says. He's already got his hat off and is running his hands over the wagon, prying at loose pieces and looking under creaking floorboards.

Henry holds up a lantern as Carr shimmies under the coach.

"What's he doing?" Tommy asks.

"What he's always done," Farley replies. "Once a thief, always a thief."

Something clanks and Henry drops to his knees to peer under the wagon.

"What is it?" Steinburn asks. We all lean in close.

Carr finishes up under the wagon and shimmies out, dirt coating him as he stands.

"Not a damn thing," he says. He tosses Steinburn an empty burlap sack and begins to dust himself off. "Most folk hide their valuables in the undercarriage."

"But not the Merriweathers," Steinburn says with a shake of his head.

I remember the day Matson came by the livery, the shadows stretching long across the dirt as he walked back up the thoroughfare into town.

"Find what you was lookin' for?" I'd asked.

"Sure did."

"Daisy." Carr's sharp voice calls me back. "Get them horses."

I fetch the Merriweather horses from the corral, checking once to make sure Willy is still tied up, then help Carr hitch them to the wagon.

Farley and Tommy climb into the bench seat and pull their revolvers out.

"Lighten up," Farley says, jostling Tommy's arm. "If we're gonna die, this is a hell of a way to go."

Tommy's face has gone ashen in the lantern light.

"Daisy, Henry, you head to the hotel," Steinburn says. "Fellas, I'll meet you at the rendezvous point. Once they're after you, just keep on running."

"Ready, Tommy boy?" Henry asks, and Tommy rolls his eyes.

"I told you not—"

"See you on the other side," Henry cuts him off with a handshake and a smile.

"Let's go," I say, and am surprised my voice doesn't shake.

Steinburn rides off into the dark, ponying Tommy's and Farley's horses behind him. He's to meet them at the drop-off point, and they'll make a quick getaway, as long as things go according to plan. Carr takes Lucky and Biscuit, and that leaves Henry and me to walk up the thoroughfare to the hotel.

He walks beside me, and when I look over he glances down with a smile. "Think you can handle this, Miss Allen?"

"Of course I can. And it's Daisy." We smile, and it helps ease my beating heart, if only for a moment.

Whores call out to Henry from the boardwalks and

balconies, enticing him with silk scarves and flashes of bare skin. He tips his hat to them as we pass, and I can almost see the disappointment in their eyes. I imagine they don't get too many good-looking fellas in their beds—Henry would be a welcome reprieve.

The hotel at the end of the thoroughfare burns bright with lantern light. The flowers on the deck are in full bloom and floral smells tickle my nose as Henry opens the door and gestures for me to step inside. Almost as soon as my dusty boots hit the floorboards, the man behind the desk lights up with a smile.

"Welcome!" he says. "How can I help you? A bath, perhaps? A room for the night?" His eyes fall on Henry as he steps in behind me.

"Just lookin' for a meal," Henry says, and his voice don't even shake.

"Of course. Please take a seat in the dining room." The man gestures to our right, where a simple dining room is bustling with activity. I quickly scan the crowd, and not a single blond head is to be found. My eyes swing up toward the second floor, where doors line a long hallway. Elizabeth must be in her room.

We expected this, figured we'd have to draw her out. Hell, we even accounted for the rough fellas crowded around tables, smoking cigarettes and playing cards.

As we find a table for two, I sit and casually glance into the room opposite the dining hall. It has a fireplace with a softly burning fire, and couches where guests can lounge. Matson and Wilkes sit on one such couch, whiskeys in hand and their eyes narrowed as they discuss something with drawn faces. Hopkins, maybe?

Since overhearing their conversation, I haven't been able to get it out of my head. If it's Hopkins who's been sabotaging their shine, then why? He had it out for Papa and for Merriweather, based on what he said that night, but why the bad blood between them? Hopefully the book will shed some light on things. I've just gotta get my hands on it first.

"Somethin' to eat?" a pretty young girl in an apron asks us.

"We'll take whatever you have," Henry says, flashing her his blue-eyed smile. Her cheeks turn a bit pink and she doesn't even bother looking in my direction before flitting off through the crowded dining room.

"Do ladies always do what you ask?"

"Hmm?" He looks over at me as though he don't know what I'm talking about, but the smile pulling on the corner of his lips says otherwise.

We each get a drink, and I sip at my whiskey slowly, watching Wilkes and Matson from across the foyer. They look around frequently, as if studying the rooms, and I always glance away, trying to keep myself from their line of sight.

The young woman delivers our food soon after, again not even looking in my direction as she puts the food down. She nearly misses the table, and I have to grab the plate before it falls in my lap.

"Why, I oughta . . ." I mumble, and she turns to face me.

"What's that, miss?"

"Another whiskey," I say, and she gives me a brief smile before turning away to fetch the drink.

"You sure about that?" Henry asks, already stuffing his mouth with corn bread. I know he ain't got money to pay for it, but here soon that shouldn't be a problem.

"I'm fine. Just need to settle my nerves, is all."

But I don't get the chance. Before she can return with my drink, gunshots split the air, sending a shocked silence through the dining room.

As we planned, Henry jumps up and runs to the window. Across the way, Matson and Wilkes put down their drinks.

"They're stealin' a coach!" Henry yells to no one in particular. People crowd the windows, pushing to see, but I keep my eyes on the Merriweathers. They go to the window just as Farley and Tommy tear by in the stolen stagecoach, their guns waving like flags as they fire bullets into the night sky.

So far so good.

My gaze shifts to the stairs as my fingers drum on the tablecloth. Any moment Elizabeth and Lily should come down those stairs, concerned about the gunshots. And when they do, I'll slip up the stairs behind them, find the book and the cash in her hotel room, and drop out the back window to where Carr is waiting in the alley below.

But Elizabeth don't come down. Only Lily does.

She steps into the foyer and Matson immediately goes to her. He takes her arm and pulls her close, whispering something into her ear. I can't hear a damn thing over the commotion, which Henry continues to stir up, and I can't see his lips moving.

Lily's eyes go wide and she nods her head once. Matson adjusts his jacket, pulls a pistol from the holster at his side, and motions for Wilkes and the other men to follow. They crowd outside just as the sheriff and his deputies go galloping by, and now's my only chance.

But this ain't how it's supposed to go. Elizabeth was supposed to come down, I was supposed to slip upstairs unnoticed. Now Lily is turning, lifting the hem of her dress to walk back up the stairs. And my chance is vanishing before my eyes.

I stand. The young girl hesitates at the entrance to the dining room, my whiskey glass in her hand. I take it and down the glass in two gulps. It burns like hellfire going down, but now my belly is warm and my inhibitions limited.

My boots are quiet on the floorboards as I slip up the stairs behind Lily and follow her down the hallway to a closed door. When she reaches for the doorknob, I step up behind her and press the barrel of my revolver to the back of her head.

CHAPTER 19
September 1880

SHE FREEZES, HER hand on the doorknob.

"Open it."

"I can—"

"Now." I press the gun more firmly against the back of her head. Part of me wants to stop, to apologize and lower the gun and beg her forgiveness, but the other part of me, the part put there by Hopkins, won't allow it. "Open the door."

Her fingers shake as she wraps them around the doorknob and twists. The door creaks open.

"Finally," comes Elizabeth's voice from somewhere in the room. "What was all that—"

She turns and looks up from her vanity as we step into the room. Her blue eyes go wide, but only for a moment. Then they narrow, and I can all but see the calculations going on inside her head.

I shut the door with my boot and Lily jumps.

"You stand real still," I tell her, "and ain't no one gonna get hurt."

"It's Daisy, right?" Elizabeth puts down her hairbrush and turns to face me. "What do you want?" Her eyes don't leave mine, almost startling in their intensity. I'd expected her to cry, to beg for Lily's life, but she don't do none of that. In fact, her pink lips don't so much as turn into a frown. Her face is completely neutral, unreadable.

"You're gonna give me the book and the money," I tell her. "And you're gonna tell me everything you know about Hopkins."

A brief moment of silence passes between us. Lily trembles.

"What use do you have for my ledger?"

"Ain't none of your business."

"But it is. It's my entire business. So why should I give it to you?" She tips her head, just barely, and a strand of blond hair slips across her shoulder.

I shift, pressing the barrel of my gun against Lily's smooth brown temple. She lets out a whimper and a single tear streaks down her cheek.

"Is that book really worth more than her life?"

Another moment of silence, this one more loaded than the last. Elizabeth's gaze shifts, only briefly, to Lily. Her lips press into a firm line. I ain't got all night.

"You've got ten seconds."

Her eyes are back on me.

"Ten. Nine. Eight."

She still don't say anything. Lily starts to cry harder.

"Seven. Six."

Fuck. Could I really pull this trigger?

"Five. Four."

"Miss," Lily whimpers. "Please."

Elizabeth doesn't move.

"Three. Two."

I grit my teeth.

"Fine."

Lily lets out an audible gasp, and I try not to do the same.

Elizabeth stands from her vanity and crosses the room. She sweeps back a rug and pries a loose floorboard up, and hiding inside is the ledger.

She tucks it under her arm, then purses her lips and studies me. "The orphan hunting down the outlaw. How interesting." Those lips turn up into a smile as she holds out the ledger. I keep the gun trained on Lily as I reach for it, but Elizabeth pulls it just out of reach. "You should know, nobody steals from the Merriweathers and gets away with it." Her eyes flick toward Lily and then back to me. "If you take this ledger, you'd best run somewhere you can't be found."

"I ain't scared of a few more enemies."

"You should be." Her smile is perfect, practiced, as she hands the ledger to me. I tuck it under my arm, still aiming at Lily's head.

"Now the money."

"I don't have it." She shrugs. "I have men to handle all that for me." The smile she gives me is more poisonous than a pit viper. "Go on, you can tear this room apart, but you aren't going to find anything." She steps aside and gestures to the tidy room. I clench my teeth.

Henry yells my name, his voice muffled by the closed door. I'm out of time.

The silver necklace at the base of Elizabeth's throat shines in the candlelight, just like it did that day in the afternoon sun.

"Give me the necklace."

Her eyes darken.

"*Now!*" I swing my gun around and point it at Elizabeth, then back at Lily. "I'll kill the *both* of you. Take it off!"

She breaks it from her neck and throws it at me, and I fumble to catch it. With the chain clasped firmly in my hand, and my gun still sweeping between the two women, I move for the door.

It's hard not to run as soon as that door closes behind me. I walk quickly down the hallway, then take the stairs to the foyer. Henry is still in the dining room, and he smiles when he sees me. But as soon as my boots hit the entryway, Wilkes steps through the front door.

His eyes meet mine, and his gaze travels down to the ledger tucked under my arm. He reaches for his gun. I don't give him the chance to take aim.

"Run!" Henry yells.

I'm already hightailing it toward the back door. People yelp and curse as I scramble down the hallway, shoving them out of the way as I go.

"Stop her!" Wilkes yells, but no one dares reach out for me. He'd already have shot me by now if not for all these people. But once I'm out that back door, I won't have no one else to protect me.

I crash through the door, barely getting it open before my shoulder collides with the wood. It sends me stumbling, but I catch myself before I face-plant in the dirt.

Taking a hard right, I sprint toward the alley where Carr is supposed to be waiting. Boots pound in the dirt behind me and a gunshot splits the night. I yelp as the bullet goes screaming past me, missing by a hair. It's a miracle it didn't take my damn ear off.

I round the corner, and there he is. As soon as Carr sees me, he reaches for his gun. For a brief moment, I falter. He aims in my direction, and my heart leaps into my throat. He fires, and Wilkes screams.

Ledger pressed to my chest, I spin around. Wilkes's hand is bleeding something fierce, and his gun lies abandoned in the dirt. Henry is right on his heels, and he crashes into Wilkes, sending him sprawling onto the ground before he scoops up his gun and continues toward us.

"Daisy!" Carr snaps. I spin around. "Let's go!"

Still holding the ledger, I climb into the saddle and take hold of Lucky's reins. Henry, wild-eyed and laughing like the devil, swings onto Biscuit and waves Wilkes's gun in the air.

I glance back. Wilkes is struggling up out of the dirt, his hand clutched to his chest.

"I'll kill you!" he screams. "I'll fucking kill you!"

We ride off, Carr leading the way. It's a damn good thing Farley and Tommy distracted the sheriff and his deputies, or else they'd be all over us by now. I just hope the boys made it to the rendezvous point before the law could catch up.

On our way out of town, my eyes land on the gunsmith and a wicked idea comes to my mind.

"Henry!" He glances over at me and I toss him the ledger.

"What the—"

"Go on, I'll catch up!"

"No!" Carr yells, glancing back over his shoulder.

But I don't listen. I turn Lucky toward the gunsmith, jump out of the saddle before he's stopped moving, and crash through the door with my gun drawn.

I'd expected to face off with the gunsmith, but the shop is empty. And there, hanging on the wall, is that pearl-handled revolver.

I scramble around the counter and snatch it off the wall. The steel is cool and smooth under my fingers, and I slip Papa's old revolver into my holster. Moonlight filters through a dusty window, illuminating the pearl and making it sparkle. I let out a low whistle.

Taking aim with the shiny new firearm, I turn toward the door and my stomach drops.

"Put it down." The gunsmith stands in the doorway, his frame silhouetted by the lantern flickering outside. He's got a double-barrel pointed right at me. "Put it down, miss. I don't wanna use this."

I don't move. My eyes dart left to right.

"Now, miss." The gunsmith cocks the double-barrel.

And a bottle shatters over his head. He goes rigid, and then he falls. His collapse sets off the shotgun, and the slugs rip through the wall beside me, sending splintered wood spinning through the air. Dust sprinkles down from overhead, pattering softly across the brim of my hat as I catch my breath. Another foot to the left and I'd have two holes blasted right through my belly.

"Now we're even," Henry says, tossing the broken bottle aside.

Heart racing, I step over the man in the doorway and hurry back outside with Henry. I'm surprised to find Carr still waiting for us, but the look on his face is damn near deadly. He don't say a word as he turns his horse around and gallops off.

"I can't believe you just did that," Henry says as we mount up.

Neither can I.

I smile to myself as we put heels to flanks and ride into the night.

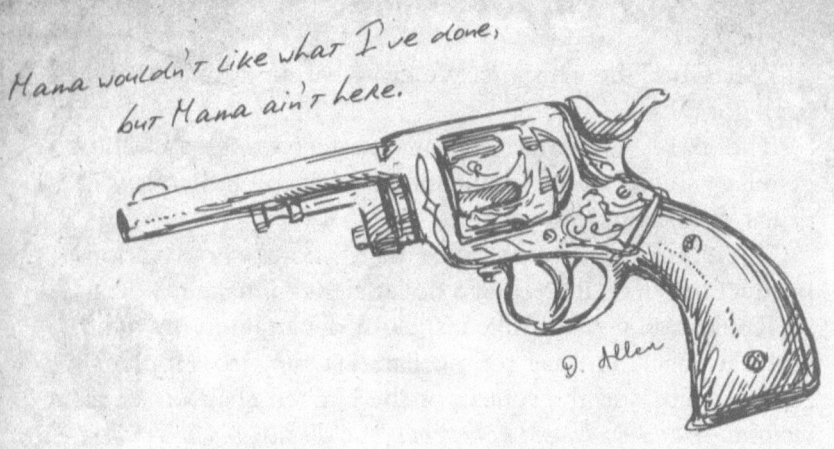

Mama wouldn't like what I've done, but Mama ain't here.

CHAPTER 20
September 1880

EVERYONE IS WAITING for us when we get back to camp. I pull Lucky to a stop and swing off his back amidst excited chatter.

My eyes find Tommy and I pull him in for a hug.

"You made it," I say.

"Just barely. That wagon near fell apart the way Farley was drivin' it."

I look around, spot Farley, and smile at him for what might be the first time. He may be a bastard, but at least he pulled this off.

"Well?" Steinburn asks, pushing through the others. "Did you get it?"

"Sure did." Henry pulls the ledger from his saddlebag with a flourish. "Behold, the holiest of bibles."

"Don't sass," Ethel says, reprimanding him with a smile.

"I'd never." He winks at her while Steinburn takes the ledger and flips through the pages.

"My God," he whispers. We crowd around him, anxious for a good look.

The pages are arranged into perfect grids, each box detailing shipments of moonshine, tobacco, and a slew of drugs, from opium to cocaine.

There are pages of shipping dates, notes about various product imports, and enough dollar signs to make me dizzy.

Realization goes off like a stick of dynamite in my mind, and I'm back in that root cellar, listening to Hopkins's gravely voice and the squeak of the kitchen chair under his weight. *"Bastard who sold us both out,"* he'd said. *"Merriweather."*

Was Hopkins involved in this? It'd be cause enough to land him in jail. But what did Papa have to do with it, and why did Merriweather sell him out?

Frustration causes my jaw to clench. I reach into my pocket and pull out Elizabeth's silver chain. If only I'd gotten more out of her than a damn necklace.

"Look here." Steinburn flips the page and points to the words scrawled across the top: *Canon City, Colorado.*

"What else does it say?" Henry leans in close and Steinburn pushes him back.

We wait in tense silence as Steinburn turns the page. His eyes shift left to right and then flick up to us.

"Fairplay, then on to Denver."

"That must be where he's headed," Henry says, clapping his hands.

"Maybe." Steinburn closes the book and tucks it under his arm. "Maybe not. But it's our best bet at getting back on his trail."

CHAPTER 21
September 1880

I TWIRL A daisy between my fingers and watch the wind dance through the tall grass. The pines stand stoic against a cloudless blue sky as I lie back and close my eyes.

The going has been rough—we near lost a wagon crossing the Arkansas, and we've a long ride through the mountains to reach Fairplay. Would be simple if we could travel the way the crow flies, but riding these narrow paths through the mountains is slowing us down considerably.

I reach for my revolvers—Papa's .45 and my new .38 with the creamy pearl handle. They feel good in my hands, like home.

Home.

I've been thinking about it lately. Hell, I ain't ever stopped thinking about it. My heart squeezed as we left Canon City behind. Each mile was a mile farther than I'd ever been from home, and I've still many miles to go.

I lift my guns to the sky, thumbs cocking the hammers, fingers resting on triggers. A month ago I'd have turned these on myself, used a bullet to put an end to my short life. But not now. Now I've Hopkins to kill.

"Daisy." Carr stands at the edge of the clearing, his hat tipped low against the afternoon sun. A yellowed poster flutters in his hand, its edges curling and snapping, beckoning me near.

"What you got there?" I ask, slipping the guns back into my holsters. That necklace I stole sold for a nice chunk of change. It weren't much, but it's kept our bellies full and our chambers loaded.

Carr don't say a word as he holds the paper out to me. I cross the clearing and take it from him, squinting against the sunlight as I lift it up to read.

And right there, clear as fucking day, is my face.

"Wanted, alive or dead," I read aloud. "Pistol Daisy, for robbery and assault in Canon City, Colorado."

My eyes flick up. Carr studies me, his face in shadow.

"Can you believe this?" I ask. "They're callin' me Pistol Daisy." I pull out a gun and smile at the way it shines in the light. "But it's a revolver."

Carr just smiles.

THE END

Look for the next book in the

PISTOL DAISY

series, *Whiskey City*, coming soon.

ACKNOWLEDGEMENTS

I have so many people to thank for helping me make *Pistol Daisy* the best it could be.

My love: Greg. You read an early draft and gave me honest feedback that helped me reshape the plot and give Daisy a voice that was both unique and authentic. Your passion for the project never failed to get me excited, and the hours you spent discussing the story and the characters with me weren't ever taken for granted. I love you!

My betas: Lynette, Matthew, Naava, Kat, Peggy, Tanna, Becca, Molly, Brooke, Jessica, Charles, Joey, Nicki, Laurel, Kevin, Rebecca, and Jason. You all read a draft that wasn't *quite* there yet and gave me valuable feedback that allowed me to transform Daisy's story into what it is today. Your kind words and gentle encouragement helped guide me as I worked on putting the final touches on the story. Thank you so much for your hard work and effort—I truly appreciate it!

My cover designer: MoorBooks Design. I couldn't be more excited about the way you were able to bring Daisy to life. I'm so glad I found you and can't wait to work together on many more books to come!

I used to think writing books was a solitary activity, and while much of the work is done alone, none of this can come together without the love and help of other passionate people. So thank you, everyone! You all mean so much to me!

ABOUT THE AUTHOR

Natalia Leigh graduated from Colorado State University
with a bachelor's degree in English and a
concentration in creative writing.

When not writing, she can usually be found playing
video games, eating vegan pizza, and editing for her clients.

You can visit her at:
www.natalialeigh.com

www.ingramcontent.com/pod-product-compliance
Lightning Source LLC
Chambersburg PA
CBHW022024170626
46808CB00003B/1047